Can't resi~~~~~~~~~~~~~~~

Then you'll love ~~~~~~~~~~

Harlequin Bl~~~~~~~~~~~~~~

continues with ~~~~ irresistible soldiers

from all branches of the armed forces.

Don't miss

COMMAND CONTROL

by Sara Jane Stone

August 2014

WICKED NIGHTS

by Anne Marsh

October 2014

BRING ME TO LIFE

by Kira Sinclair

December 2014

Blaze®

Dear Reader,

I am so excited to share Logan's story with you! Army Ranger Logan Reed was one of the horse soldiers from my Harlequin Blaze debut, *Command Performance*. He appeared as a side character, but I could not stop thinking about the lonely widower sidelined from the job he loved. I felt he deserved a happily-ever-after. But first, I needed to find the perfect heroine.

Then I met Sadie, the erotica writer determined to succeed. I love writing about strong women, but what made Sadie stand out in my mind was her constant struggle for work/life balance. Sadie seemed like a great match for Logan—except for the fact that he is on a mission to keep a low profile and she is actively seeking publicity for the next book in her bestselling erotica series.

I love hearing from readers! Could you relate to Sadie's desire to balance her personal life with her career ambitions? Did you enjoy the small-town setting? Let me know! Find me on Facebook or drop by my website, www.sarajanestone.com, and while you're there don't forget to sign up for my newsletter to receive information about new releases, contests and more.

Happy reading!

Sara Jane Stone

Command Control

—

Sara Jane Stone

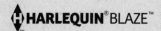

Recycling programs
for this product may
not exist in your area.

ISBN-13: 978-0-373-79813-1

COMMAND CONTROL

Copyright © 2014 by Sara Jane Stone

Printed in U.S.A.

www.Harlequin.com

ABOUT THE AUTHOR

After several years on the other side of the publishing industry, Sara Jane Stone bid goodbye to her sales career to pursue her dream—writing romance novels. Armed with a firm belief that dreams do come true, she sat down at her keyboard to write fun, sexy stories like the ones she loved to read. Sara Jane currently resides in Brooklyn, New York, with her very supportive real-life hero, two lively young children and a lazy Burmese cat. Visit her online at www.sarajanestone.com, become a fan of Sara Jane Stone on Facebook or follow her on Twitter, @sarajanestone.

Books by Sara Jane Stone

HARLEQUIN BLAZE
770—COMMAND PERFORMANCE

To Maya, for her help plotting this book.

And to my husband, thank you for your endless support and love. I couldn't have written this book without you!

The things he wants, they are dirty—depraved even—but then so are my fantasies. The difference is he knows how to ask for what he wants, and I lost my voice long ago.
>　　　*—Isabelle's Command: Possession, Volume 1*
>　　　　　　*by MJ Lane*

"Don't leave," he says. This time, his words are not an ultimatum. "Tell me what you want. Anything. I am yours to command."
>　　　*—Isabelle's Command: Submission, Volume 2*
>　　　　　　*by MJ Lane*

I found my voice. But now, my heart is exposed. And I don't know if I'm ready to love him.
>　　　*—Isabelle's Command: Control, Volume 3*
>　　　　*by MJ Lane (A Work In Progress)*

1

"Every woman in here is staring at you."

U.S. Army Ranger Logan Reed looked up from his burger at the petite, white-haired woman across the table. Fact was he would rather be anywhere—Iraq, Afghanistan, a remote African village—but here, sitting across the table from his aunt Lou at The Quilted Quail, an old barn that had been converted into the only respectable restaurant in Mount Pleasant, Vermont.

"Because they want to raffle me off at the Summer Festival." He returned his attention to his food. After a week spent hiking and camping, he'd thought a decent meal would be worth venturing into town for an early dinner. Now, he wasn't so sure.

"You can't hide from the people who have known you since you were in diapers. Look, there's Cindy." Aunt Lou waved her hand at the blond-haired, blue-eyed first-grade teacher. "She was asking when you'd be back from your trip. She is in charge of this year's raffle and she thinks 'lunch with a hero' will be a big-ticket item."

"I'm not a goddamn hero."

"Language, Logan," his aunt scolded.

He watched as Cindy weaved through the wooden tables. He'd been approached by nearly everyone who had anything to do with the town's Summer Festival since his commanding officer had ordered him to take some time to rest, relax and get his head on straight. After Logan's mistake had left his teammate with a bullet in the shoulder, he couldn't blame his CO. And now that a journalist wanted to write a book about the mission Logan had screwed up? The army had even more reason to keep him on R & R.

Active duty Special Forces soldiers did not give interviews. Press, good or bad, hindered his team's ability to do their jobs. His team, like many of the other elite units, was designed to slip into an area unnoticed, execute their task and leave undetected. Sometimes, their missions required them to blend in with the local population without alerting the enemy. They wore their hair longer than the average military buzz cut. Some of the guys grew beards. And at times, they worked alongside the good guys in the area. If the media put their names and faces out there, along with their rank and job description, the enemy would see it and there was a chance it would handicap their future missions.

Not to mention the fact that nine times out of ten, the press focused on their mistakes, not their wins. His team had completed hundreds of successful missions, but the only one anyone wanted to write about was the one that had gone south. His CO was determined to make sure that didn't happen.

Logan was ready and willing to do his part and lie low in rural Vermont. His job as a Ranger—it was everything to him. This time, when Logan returned to his team, he would be ready for duty—no distractions. That meant he needed to put his grief to rest.

He'd never forget. Not by a long shot. But he didn't need to feel like he was drowning in loss every damn day. Jane had been gone for over a year now. At some point, he had to put the past behind him.

But thanks to his friends and family, he felt more bound to his memories than ever. They had good intentions. Still, everyone treated him as if he was supposed to spend the rest of his life immersed in sorrow. Unless he was on the battlefield. Out there they assumed he could do no wrong, as if putting on the uniform transformed him into some sort of idol. That's why he'd gone hiking in the first place, to get away from the town determined to label him a freaking hero.

"I agreed to come to town for a burger," he said. "Nothing else."

"If we always got what we wanted out of life," Aunt Lou said, "I'd be living in one of those fancy homes like the ladies on *The Real Housewives*."

And he'd be back with his team doing the job he loved instead of sidelined indefinitely. Or better yet, Jane would still be alive and he wouldn't have spent the past year feeling like everyone in his life was tiptoeing around him. He didn't need an endless pity party.

The smell of Cindy's floral perfume reached the table first. Logan glanced at the door, debating whether to abandon his burger.

"Mind your manners," Aunt Lou ordered as Cindy followed her perfume cloud to their table.

Logan stood, allowing Cindy to wrap her arms around him.

"Logan, it's so good to see you out." Cindy drew back and looked at him, her brow furrowed. "How are you?"

God, how he hated those three little words. "Just fine, ma'am."

He reclaimed his seat and his burger. Without waiting

for an invitation, Cindy pulled a chair from an empty table and sat down next to him.

"Have you given any more thought to the raffle? The people of Mount Pleasant would be lining up to buy tickets if they knew the grand prize was lunch with our very own U.S. Army ranger. Everyone is dying to learn more about your latest mission." Cindy dropped her voice to a near whisper, leaning in until the scent of her perfume left him practically gagging. "Especially after seeing that picture in the paper."

She wasn't the first person in town to reference the picture that had spread like wildfire through the nation's media. The image showed Logan and his teammates riding horses provided by an Afghan warlord, their faces thankfully obscured by handkerchiefs. "That's classified."

"Surely you can share some of the details," Cindy pressed. "Perhaps over lunch with the raffle winner? All the proceeds go to the school's literacy program."

Logan reached for his beer and took a long drink, wishing like hell he could get up and leave. He had a hunch the raffle winner would be a woman—the men in town wouldn't be caught dead on a lunch date with him—and she wouldn't be interested in the nitty-gritty details of his latest mission.

Since he'd been home, a number of single women had tried to cozy up to him, always proclaiming how sorry they were for his loss while trying to drop subtle hints they were interested if he was ready to start dating again. It was plain weird.

Logan glanced at the door. Too bad he couldn't call for an extraction team and fast-rope out of there. But walking away wouldn't stop Cindy from trying any tactic to get a commitment out of him. He gave his aunt a pleading look.

"Cindy, you know he can't talk about the details of his

missions." His aunt stood and took Cindy's arm. "I think I saw Suzanne Hummel on the patio, and I need to speak with her about the band she hired to play at Summer Festival."

"Of course." Cindy turned to him, dropping her voice low. "Promise me you'll think about the raffle. We need an answer soon. The festival is only days away."

Aunt Lou pulled Cindy away, but they were still within earshot when Lou called over her shoulder, "If you leave first, do me a favor and move the small desk in the library down to the guesthouse."

Logan nodded. He had every intention of ducking out as soon as he finished his burger. He'd driven his truck here knowing he might need to escape before his aunt. "Sure. After I feed the cows."

"Before," his aunt insisted. "I have a tenant arriving today and she's a writer. Asked if we could provide a space for her to work."

Logan frowned. A writer—specifically a journalist— was the reason he was on forced R & R. "A writer? What kind?"

"She didn't say, but you can ask her yourself when she arrives." Aunt Lou walked away, taking Cindy with her. "And think about the raffle, Logan."

Logan turned his attention back to his burger. He had nothing against raising money for literacy, but posing as a hero? It made him feel like a hypocrite. Yes, he'd ridden a horse through Taliban country. Big deal. He'd also been so damn distracted when his team had gone in to rescue the three female aid workers held captive in a remote region of Afghanistan that he'd forgotten to cover his teammate. One inch in another direction and that bullet would have hit the woman in Hunter's arms. It had practically brushed the top of her head.

No, he couldn't sit down to lunch and recount his heroics. He was biding his time in Mount Pleasant, helping his aunt with the farm, until he could return to work. It killed him, sitting on his hands, away from the action. But he knew he deserved the punishment. And this time when he went back, he needed to have his head in the game 100 percent.

Still, his team was like family. Aside from Aunt Lou, the only one he had left. Being away from them—the loneliness ate at him.

Logan shook away the thought and returned to his burger. Across the restaurant, the door opened, letting in a shaft of midday summer sunlight. A redhead with mile-long legs walked in and headed for the bar that ran the length of the barn-turned-restaurant.

He studied the mysterious woman as she moved across the restaurant with carefree confidence. In one hand, she held a spiral notebook and a small purse. She was new to town, probably a tourist, though she didn't look like the type to spend her free time hiking and biking. Her high-heeled sandals screamed big city.

Her loose curls bounced with each step, the bright red a sharp contrast to her creamy white skin. And her green eyes shone with playful mystery, as if she had a secret she wanted to whisper in his ear. Everything about her was vivid, fresh and exciting.

His gaze returned to her legs, narrowing on the point where they disappeared beneath her black miniskirt.

If you think her skirt is too short, she's too young for you. His teammate wasn't with him tonight, but Mike's familiar mantra echoed in Logan's mind. One of his T-shirts would cover more of her legs. He closed his eyes. And, great, an image of the redhead in his army T-shirt was now planted in his mind.

Logan forced himself to look away. She was too young

for him. Not that thirty-five was ancient, but the word *widower* made a man seem older than his years.

He took one last look as the redhead slid onto a stool at the end of the bar. She'd chosen a seat close to his table and the proximity offered an up-close view as she crossed her legs, the indecent skirt sliding a little higher. Too young and too wild. Logan turned away, praying no one saw the longing in his eyes.

If he was being honest with himself, what he really wanted was a few nights of hot and heavy sex to take the edge off his loneliness. Nothing serious. Just something physical to make him feel alive.

Logan caught the waiter's eye and signaled for the check. While he waited, his gaze drifted back to the woman.

He watched as she accepted a glass of red wine and opened her notebook. She took a sip, but her eyes never moved from the words in front of her. Setting the glass down, she drew her lower lip into her mouth and ran her teeth over it. She made reading look like a forbidden act, something that should be done behind closed doors.

The waiter returned and Logan opened up his wallet. Then he stood and headed for the door. He had to get out of here. Longing and loneliness would not change the fact that any reasonable woman would expect things he wasn't ready to deliver.

2

"Seduce me. I want to feel your hands on me. Your mouth, your tongue. I want to feel every inch of you holding me down, claiming me," I say as I lean back on the bed. *"That's an order."*

Sadie read the words for a third time, but failed to reach the next paragraph. She couldn't concentrate on the pages she'd written yesterday. Not with a man staring at her. Reading a sex scene in public was nothing new. In Manhattan, she'd reviewed her chapters while riding the subway. Before she'd sold her first book, commuting to and from her multiple waitressing jobs was when she'd done most of her writing.

But reading while a stranger watched her as if he wanted to devour her? That destroyed her focus and sent parts of her body spiraling toward take-me-now excitement.

Sadie shifted in her seat. His attention—and her response—reminded her how much her body missed her ex and their regular bedroom workouts, even if her mind had moved on quickly in the wake of their parting three months earlier. But the interest she felt had nothing to do with the past.

She looked up from her notebook as the stranger walked

by her bar stool. With his wavy dark brown hair, piercing brown eyes and muscles even his cargo shorts and loose black T-shirt couldn't hide, the man defined ruggedly handsome.

She turned her head to one side, her eyes narrowing. He seemed strangely familiar. Studying his backside as he walked toward the door, she knew. Mr. Ruggedly Handsome looked like Hugh Jackman when he'd played Wolverine in the X-Men movies—minus the facial hair—from his serious expression to his ready-for-battle body.

He walked with grace and purpose. Part of her wanted to go after him, find out if he was available and interested. But she couldn't. Not right now. Her sister would be here any second. As long as she was in Mount Pleasant, her family came first. Everything else, from work to droolworthy strangers, needed to take a backseat.

The door opened and he disappeared into the sunshine, leaving Sadie to her reading.

"There you are." Laurel, Sadie's twin, enveloped her in a big hug. They might have been born the same day, but the similarities ended there. Sadie had inherited their father's Irish coloring, while Laurel looked like the all-American girl next door with her blond hair and blue eyes. A very pregnant girl next door.

"Careful, you'll crush the baby," Sadie said, struggling to maintain her balance on the barstool.

Laurel squeezed tighter. "I can't believe you're here."

"You said you needed me."

"I know. And you always come through for me. But this time you're *here.* For a whole month. I never thought you'd leave New York for that long."

"I can barely believe it myself."

An entire month in small-town Vermont, away from the hustle and bustle of her everyday life in New York City, away from sushi delivered to her doorstep, away from her quiet writing space. Of course, she could work here. She could write anywhere. But still, she was here. For Laurel. For once, she was trying to put her sister first, to tip the scale between personal life and professional.

"Sit. Please," Sadie said, pulling away from her twin's embrace. "You look like you should be resting with your feet up. You're…"

"Enormous?" Laurel said with a wide grin.

"That wasn't the word I was looking for."

"Only for another month." Her sister took her hand and squeezed. "I can't believe you'll be here when the baby arrives. I asked Dad to come up, too, but he said the trip was too expensive."

Sadie frowned, her wineglass hovering close to her lips. "I sent him an extra check with a note to buy a plane ticket."

"Oh, well, he didn't mention it," Laurel said, the excitement in her eyes dimming.

Damn him, Sadie thought. Her father might begrudge her charity, but he didn't have to take it out on Laurel. As far as Sadie was concerned the monthly checks weren't a handout. Their father had worked hard to provide for his twin girls after their mother had passed away when they were babies. Now it was Sadie's turn to take care of him. She had the money to ensure they stayed afloat. And with the way her book had taken off, she could do a lot more than pay the bills. But her father and sister would only accept so much.

Laurel shrugged. "It's just as well. I don't know where I'd put him. We barely have room for you and the baby."

Sadie set her wineglass on the bar. "I found someplace else to stay."

Laurel's brow furrowed. "You're staying with us. After

all you've done for us, the checks you sent when I lost my job, we owe you. I can't repay the money, but I can feed and house you for the next month. Please, Sadie. Let me do this for you. I promise to bake your favorite cookies."

"I'd be in the way on your couch." Laurel and her husband rented a cramped one-bedroom cottage outside of town. And while Sadie lived in a Manhattan apartment the size of a shoe box—albeit one with a Central Park view—it had been years since she'd shared her living space with her twin. They'd fought day and night back then. She couldn't imagine it would be better now that Laurel was eight months pregnant.

"I saw an ad online for a guesthouse rental on the neighboring farm," she continued. "I called and it was available. This way you will have some time with Greg before the baby arrives and I will have space to write. I have a book due soon."

"Lou's guesthouse?"

Sadie nodded. "I spoke with a woman named Louise Reed."

"Everyone calls her Lou."

"Well, I'm staying in Lou's guesthouse," Sadie said firmly. "But that does not change the fact that I'm here for you. I'm going to be the best big sister."

"You're five minutes older. I don't think that counts," Laurel said, her eyes brimming with tears. It was an old argument. One they'd joked about for years. "But thank you," her twin added. "For everything. I appreciate the money. We wouldn't have survived without it. Still, having you here means even more to me. And one day, I'm going to find a way to repay you. When you need me, I'll be there. I promise."

Those heartfelt words sent a wave of guilt crashing down on her. She was here for her sister. Mostly.

She glanced around the spacious restaurant, unable to meet her twin's gaze. Everything about the place was quaint and welcoming. At the back, they'd kept the old sliding door from when the building had been a barn. High up in the A-frame ceiling, light poured in through long horizontal windows. This place was a world away from her life in Manhattan. But when she went back, her life wouldn't be the same. Not even close.

"You don't have to feel guilty," Laurel said, as if reading her mind. Sadie had never been able to hide anything from her twin. It was a little scary how easily Laurel knew what Sadie was thinking. But the connection did not run both ways, which was just plain unfair.

"I know you had to get away before the world learns about your secret identity," Laurel continued.

In a few weeks, everyone would know she'd written the erotica novel everyone was talking about—*Isabelle's Command* by MJ Lane. Sadie would be on national TV promoting the release of the second book in the series. She felt a wave of excitement just thinking about it.

But two weeks earlier, a small problem had threatened her carefully planned reveal. She'd caught a photographer outside her building when she'd gone out for a bagel. Thankfully, she'd spotted him first and quickly covered her face with her arms. She'd heard the camera's click, click, click, but knew he'd only caught shots of a faceless red-haired woman walking into her building.

Of course, he'd still tried to save his story by calling her publicist to verify the woman in the pictures was MJ Lane before printing them. Her publicist had lied, telling the man no. But not all of them would fact-check. If she wasn't careful, she would not be able to keep her secret until the release of her second book. Another tabloid reporter might run the story on a hope and a prayer that the facts were correct.

Telling the world Sadie Bannerman was MJ Lane—it would happen. And she was determined to make the most of the story. This was her career, her future, her everything.

But it needed to unfold according to her plan. Here, in rural Vermont, there was very little chance her secret would get out before her next book release. Her big disclosure would be perfect.

Almost.

Once the world learned who she was, she knew her relationships, already strained from the time and energy she poured into her work, would be marked with a big fat F for *failure*. She'd have less time for her sister. And her father? She hadn't asked him, but she had a hunch he didn't like the idea of the whole world knowing she wrote erotica. He acted as if taking the money she made from her work was a cardinal sin.

She might not be able to set things right with her dad in the next few weeks, but she could take this opportunity to be here for her sister. Laurel needed her and this time sending a check to help cover the bills wasn't enough.

"It means so much to me that you'll be here when the baby arrives." The tears were no longer brimming; they were flowing down Laurel's face.

"Oh, no, don't you start. If you cry, we'll both be a weeping mess in minutes, and I refuse to cry in public. I'm here for a whole month. We're going to have some fun together before my little niece arrives." Sadie caught the bartender's attention. "Do you have pie?"

When they were little, pie had been the family cure-all. Their dad had never known what to do with two crying girls, so he'd decided it was best to splurge on a trip to the diner for a slice or two.

"Yes, dear," the man old enough to be her grandfather said. "Apple, cherry and Maine blueberry."

"Apple," Laurel said quickly.

He nodded. "Two slices?"

"No," Sadie said. "We're going to need the whole pie."

3

AFTER MORE THAN a decade in the army, Logan knew when
to withdraw and wait for the enemy to pass. Not that the
pack of elementary school teachers were hostiles, but after
his encounter with Cindy two days earlier, he wasn't taking any chances. He hadn't planned on leaving the farm,
but his aunt was driving him crazy, constantly badgering
him about the raffle.

Logan spotted the women leaving the coffee shop on
Main Street before they saw him, and his training kicked
in. Opening the door to the one-hundred-and-something-
year-old Victorian house that had been converted into
Main Street Books, he slipped inside. A covert entrance
except for the jingling bell attached to the door announcing his presence. He found a position in the rear corner of
the store, deep in the maze of bookshelves. The only window in this section looked out on a side alley lined with
garbage cans. No one would spot him back here. Pulling
the nearest book from the shelf, he pretended to read the
back cover.

"If you need assistance picking out a romance novel,
I can help."

His gaze snapped to the woman standing two feet

away holding a book in each hand—the redhead from The Quilted Quail. She'd traded in her miniskirt for a pair of jean shorts, but that didn't affect his reaction. The desire he'd felt when he'd first seen her returned full force.

"But if it's your first time—" she continued, placing the books back on the shelf "—you might want to steer clear of erotica."

"Erotica?" Logan glanced at the book in his hand. On the front cover was a practically nude woman lying on a bed. A man in leather pants stood next to her, holding a whip. It looked like an image out of a men's magazine, not something he'd find on the shelf in his hometown. "Mount Pleasant sells erotica?"

"Not much," she said grimly. "But what they do have is pretty good."

She stepped toward him, close enough for him to smell a hint of her soft floral scent—not overpowering, but enticing—and reached for a book on the shelf above his head. The side of her breast brushed his arm, sending a red-alert signal through his body.

"If you're looking for a classic romance, this is one of my favorites." She held out a copy of a Jane Austen novel.

He shook his head. "Read that one in high school. It wasn't for me."

She placed the book on the shelf and turned to him, her eyes sparkling with amusement. "To find the perfect romance, I'll need to know a little bit more about you."

Was she hitting on him? It had been so long since he'd played that game, he wasn't sure of his next move.

Tired of sitting on the sidelines waiting for his life to restart, he decided to take a chance. What was the worst thing that could happen? She'd walk away leaving him with a hard-on he wasn't sure he was ready to act on? At least he'd have felt something other than loneliness and grief.

"Not much to tell. I'm home on leave."

"You're a soldier?" Her smile widened. "Let me guess. Special Forces."

He shifted his weight from one foot to the other. He couldn't tell from her reaction if she was one of those women who jumped into bed with a man because he wore a uniform or ran in the other direction. Part of him hoped it was the former. "Army ranger."

"No kidding?" Laughing, she scanned the shelves before selecting another paperback. "This one should be just right for you."

She handed him the book. The cover showed a man's naked chest with dog tags hanging around his neck.

"He's a soldier, a SEAL, and she's a nurse," she said. "They have hot sex, overcome a few challenges and fall in love."

"The hot sex part sounds good." He set the book back on the shelf. "But I'm not looking for a fairy-tale ending."

She handed him back the first book. "Then maybe you should stick with erotica."

Her fingers brushed his, sending shock waves through his body. He let her hand linger a moment, not wanting to let the feeling go. Logan glanced up at her and saw the heat in her eyes. He knew he'd made the right call. Whatever was happening here wasn't one-sided.

He shook his head. "I'm not into whips."

"So just hot sex?" She turned back to the bookshelf and he instantly missed the physical connection. He wanted her hands on him and it didn't matter where.

He watched her index finger tap her lips as she scanned the books. His gaze zeroed in on her mouth and for a second all he could think about was what she would taste like.

"Just sex," he managed.

"I'm sure we can do better than 'just sex.' Don't you

want to leave yourself open to new experiences? We can find something wild that doesn't include whips."

"Don't think I'm ready for that," he said truthfully. He was in uncharted territory—flirting with a mysterious stranger. He should probably walk away now before it went any further.

But his feet refused to move. Excitement and anticipation pumped through him for the first time since he'd set foot in Mount Pleasant. If he couldn't ship out with his team, maybe this was the next-best thing.

"But plain old hot sex I can handle," he added, praying that wasn't a lie.

She hesitated for the first time since he'd entered the store. Had he said the wrong thing? Gone too far?

"Are you going to walk away without telling me your name because I'm not into whips?" he asked, hoping to spark the laughter he'd seen in her eyes just moments ago.

"What if I told you I could convince you to give it a try?" The uncertainty disappeared, but hell if her expression wasn't serious.

"Are you really into—"

"No, I was teasing. Whips aren't my thing," she said smiling. "And I'm Sadie."

"Logan." He ran a hand up and down the back of his neck. "But now I'm kind of curious how you'd convince me."

Sadie laughed. The sound was like a drug. It drew him in and left him wanting more.

"I'd start by reading to you." She took the book from his hands and opened to the middle.

"'That's right, baby,'" she read. "'Harder. Please.'"

He didn't think it was possible for him to get more turned on, but the combination of her husky voice and bright, laughing expression took him up a notch. Given that her eyes were fixed on the book, he didn't think she'd noticed.

But that hadn't stopped him from picking up on her response. His gaze swept over her, settling on her breasts. Either she was freezing in the unair-conditioned store or her nipples were begging for attention.

"'I want you to drive your hard…'"

She looked up at him, catching him with his gaze locked on her chest. Shit. He quickly looked away.

"Too much for a morning reading at Main Street Books?"

"No," he said with a dry laugh, running a hand through his hair. "It is just that I haven't done this in a while. Flirting."

She nodded, closing the book. "Just got out of a relationship?"

"Something like that. I'm a—"

He couldn't say the word. For the first time in months someone had looked at him with something other than pity. If he said the word *widower* the laughter would vanish. And then she'd leave. He might not be sure where this was going, but he didn't want her to disappear.

It had been over a year since he'd lost his wife to cancer. Before she'd slipped away, she'd been sick. For eighteen long months, his world had revolved around illness, pain, loss and pity—even from his teammates. Not a hint of laughter.

He wanted to move forward. After his last mission, he didn't have a choice. His grief had distracted him at the worst possible moment. He needed to add some lightness back into his life.

"It's a long story," he added.

She turned her head to one side, studying him. "One that explains why you're hiding from a group of women?"

He blinked. "How did you know?"

"I saw your covert entrance and the group of ladies across the street. Pretty sneaky. Although next time you might want to choose the nonfiction section." Her tone was friendly, but no longer teasing. "Why are they after you?"

"I'll tell you," he said, determined to hear her laugh again. "But first, I need your word you won't join forces with them."

She lowered her voice as if they were discussing a top-secret mission. "I promise."

"They're trying to raffle me off to the highest bidder."

Sadie let out a bark of laughter, raising her hand to her mouth. "And you're not for sale?"

"No, ma'am." He shook his head. "But those women? Man, they're relentless. If my team found out? I'd never be able to live that one down."

The bell over the door rang. Sadie stepped back and peered around the last bookshelf in the section. From there, he suspected she could see the front door.

"They're in the store." She returned to the romance/erotica section and scooped up her purse. "We need to get you out of here. We can't have a tough soldier like you become the laughingstock of your team."

She took his hand and pulled him along behind her. "Come with me. I'm parked out back."

Hand in hand, Logan followed her through the bookshelf maze. He knew they weren't in any real danger, but his heart raced. What would this wild, sexy woman do next?

Sadie froze midaisle. If his training hadn't kicked in, he would have crashed into her, probably sending them both to the floor. As it was, she'd left him off balance.

Without warning, she pressed him against a side door

between two bookshelves. He caught himself before the shock of her body against his sent them both tumbling.

"Someone's coming," she whispered.

Instinctively, he grabbed her by the waist and pulled her around, shielding her from view, or enemy fire. But this was a bookstore in Vermont, not a war zone. Still, he didn't step away.

Her breasts pressed against his chest, sending his racing heart into overdrive. Her lower body fit between his splayed legs. With her heeled sandals and long legs, he would only need to lift her another inch before sliding inside—if they were naked and he was ready. At the moment, he only had one of the two working in his favor.

When he was on a mission, the adrenaline sometimes left him standing at attention. A hazard of the job. But right now it had everything to do with the woman staring up at him as if she couldn't wait for his next move. She shifted, rocking her hips against him. There was no way she could miss the hard evidence of just how turned on he was.

Her gaze drifted to his lips, an invitation to taste. Logan groaned, lowering his head until their lips were practically touching. And he hesitated. Releasing her waist, he ran his hands through her loose wavy hair, his eyes roaming over her parted lips. He wanted to kiss her. But not here. Not like this.

She pushed up on her tiptoes, making every muscle in his body aware of just how much he wanted her. Turning her head, she brought her mouth to his ear and whispered, "I think the coast is clear. On three, let's make a break for it. My car is the blue Prius on the left. Ready?"

He nodded, relieved and at the same time wishing the full-body contact wouldn't end.

"One, two, three," she said.

He stepped away, letting her slip in front of him and lead the way to their escape car.

This was crazy, but right now he didn't care. He felt alive and more turned on than he'd been in years—a helluva long way from that lonely cliff's edge he'd been standing on for months.

SADIE PEELED OUT of the parking lot with Mr. Ruggedly Handsome in her passenger seat. Her hands gripped the wheel, her body tense with excitement. But as soon as they turned onto the main road, guilt crept up on her. She'd come to Vermont for her sister, not to "rescue" hot soldiers from a crowd of women—especially one still reeling from a recent breakup or worse.

God, what if he was married? Sadie took her eyes off the road long enough to glance at his ring finger. Bare. She let out a breath of relief.

Still, there was a story behind that brief moment of hesitation she'd witnessed earlier. If she had to guess, a complex one. Sadie had enough problematic relationships in her life right now. If—and that was a pretty big *if*—she decided to have a vacation fling, it wouldn't be with a complicated man.

But Logan was a walking five-alarm fire. The anticipation of that almost-kiss had left her body on edge. She tightened her grip on the steering wheel. Turning left, she drove the length of the block, and turned left again.

"Mind telling me where we're going?" he asked.

"Back to the parking lot," she said. "I think the coast is clear by now. And to set the record straight, I'm not in the habit of kidnapping men I meet in bookstores."

Out of the corner of her eye, she saw Logan nod. "Go straight up ahead and turn left at the next stop sign. That will get you back there. The one-way streets here are like a maze."

"You're from the area?"

"Born and raised," he said. "Where are you visiting from?"

"Manhattan."

"Long way from home," he said.

Distancewise it was a few hours by car, but after forty-eight hours in Mount Pleasant, her home felt like a far-away world.

"My sister is having a baby." Sadie turned right, pulling in beside a large blue truck. "She asked me to come up and lend her a hand."

She put the car in Park and turned to him. Tension radiated off Mr. Ruggedly Handsome. His mouth formed a thin, grim line. The playful, teasing man she'd seen in the bookstore had vanished.

"You're the writer," he said. "The one renting Lou's guesthouse."

Sadie smiled. "Word travels fast."

"Small town." Logan opened the door. With one foot on the pavement, he turned to her. "Thanks for the rescue. And to set the record straight, I'm not in the habit of letting beautiful women kidnap me."

His words warmed her body. "Beautiful, huh?"

"I should be going."

His gaze dropped to her mouth. Remembering their almost-kiss between the shelves? The heat in his eyes said yes. But she also saw regret. Maybe he'd meant what he'd said earlier in the store—he wasn't ready. Perhaps the past still had a hold on him?

Logan exited the car, careful not to slam her door. He gave a little wave and then disappeared across the lot.

"Well, that's a first." She put the car in Reverse. She'd

never had a man almost kiss her, call her beautiful and then disappear *before* he found out what she wrote.

Sadie turned onto the main road. She could always ask Laurel about the handsome soldier, but she didn't want gossip. She'd rather hear his story from him. There was something about the longing she saw in his eyes when he looked at her. It left her wanting to do more than read sex scenes to him. She wanted to get to know him in bed and out, learn his secrets and unlock his mysteries.

4

"You're hovering." Laurel stood in front of the stove, a wooden spoon in one hand, the other resting on her belly.

"You should sit down." Sadie plucked the utensil from her twin's hand. "Rest. You've been standing over that stove all morning."

"We need food," her twin protested.

"I just filled your fridge with groceries yesterday." Sadie had been horrified when she'd looked through her sister's kitchen and realized her twin was barely getting by foodwise. She knew Laurel and her husband had been struggling since Laurel had lost her job, but Sadie sent money every month despite Laurel's protests. Her very pregnant sister should not be living off mac and cheese.

"I need to fill the freezer. Once the baby comes I won't feel like cooking. And we can't live on takeout up here like you do in New York." Laurel snatched the spoon back and turned away from Sadie.

"Greg can cook for you. Isn't that part of a husband's job after the baby comes?"

Laurel snorted. "He's not allowed in my kitchen. But even if I did let him in, he won't have the time, between work and the baby—"

"Wait, Greg's not taking time off?"

"He can't afford to. As it is they've cut his hours at the plant back to thirty-two. That's how we lost our benefits."

"I told you I'd pay the hospital bills. If you need more so Greg can stay for a week or two, the money is yours. I have more than enough to cover whatever you need, especially after this next book comes out."

"No. He can't risk losing his job. I appreciate the offer. So does Greg. But we can't turn to you for everything. We're trying to get back on our feet. If Greg does well, if he works hard and gets promoted, we'll have benefits again. And when the baby's old enough, I'm going to find another job," Laurel said, stirring briskly.

"I know you're trying. Greg, too," she said. "But you're about to have a baby. He should be home with you in the beginning."

"I'll have you here," Laurel said. "I won't need him."

"I'm here now. Why don't you let me finish that while you sit down?" Sadie made another grab for the spoon only to have her hand slapped away.

"I need to cook. And you're worse than Greg in the kitchen. Go. Write. Enjoy the peace and quiet. Your hovering is driving me batty."

Sadie closed her eyes and groaned in frustration. Three days. She had been in town for seventy-two hours and they were already making each other crazy. A month would be torture unless she started focusing on her book.

"Promise me you will rest after this casserole is in the oven," Sadie said, "and I'll leave you alone until dinner."

"Scout's honor."

Sadie pursed her lips. "We were never Girl Scouts, Laurel."

"I know." Her twin waved the spoon at the screen door. "Out. Be back at seven for dinner."

Sadie marched down the squeaky wooden steps and into the yard. She'd walked over. After living in Manhattan, it seemed odd to drive the equivalent of a few city blocks to visit her sister. She moved through Laurel's overgrown backyard, not slowing down when she reached the mowed field indicating Aunt Lou's farm. Following the fence line to the cow pasture, she headed for the red wooden barn. Her cute, quaint guesthouse stood on the other side of the cows' home.

Sadie studied the barn as she approached. The building shone like a freshly washed fire truck in the midday sun. Someone had painted it recently. The metal gate at the front of the barn swung open. Sadie froze.

Mr. Ruggedly Handsome, the man who wanted "just hot sex, no whips," walked out carrying a bucket. If she believed in fate, she would have thanked her lucky stars for depositing him on her doorstep. But she'd stopped believing in fairy godmothers and magic wands years ago. And destiny? It had never handed her anything. Her career, her success—those she chalked up to hard work and drive. No, it wasn't fate; it was coincidence, and an opportunity to learn more about him.

Sadie watched him set the bucket down. Jeans hugged the backside she'd admired that first afternoon at The Quilted Quail and a gray army T-shirt showed off his muscular arms. Leaving the gate open, he disappeared inside. When he came back, he carried two more large blue buckets, his biceps flexing from the exertion.

Sadie bit her lip. She could return to her desk in the guesthouse and write, or she could offer to help Mr. Ruggedly Handsome with his buckets. Her brain didn't even have a chance to vote before her legs started moving toward the barn.

She had hours to kill before dinner. She couldn't think

of a better way to spend her day than working alongside Logan, drawing him into conversation. She wanted to see him laugh again. He'd been full of humor at the bookstore, teasing her in the stacks. Then, one quick drive around town and he'd become withdrawn and quiet. Any woman in her shoes would be curious.

"Hi, stranger," she said, offering him a smile.

Logan stopped a few feet outside the barn, but he held on to the buckets, which suited her fine. She didn't mind seeing his muscles in action. His gaze ran down her body, taking in her plain black tank top, jean shorts that skimmed the tops of her thighs and slip-on canvas flats. Maybe not the best outfit for the farm.

But then he looked her straight in the eyes. Not a hint of disapproval there. No, she was willing to bet her next book advance that the soldier-turned-farmhand liked what he saw.

"Sadie." The way he said her name—it was as if he'd expected to run into her. He paused before adding, "Good to see you again."

She smiled. "I'm renting the guesthouse. If you're working here now, soldier, you might be seeing a lot of me."

"Lou is my aunt."

Her smiled faded. He could have mentioned that in the car. Was that why he'd pulled away?

"I'm helping her out while I'm home," he added.

"Need a hand?"

"I'm good. Just watering cows," he said. "I don't want to keep you."

He turned to the fields. The water in the buckets sloshed up the sides with each step. Sadie fell in beside him. She wasn't going to let him get away. Not this time.

"Laurel kicked me out. I could write, but I'd rather procrastinate and enjoy the fresh air." She moved closer and that sharp need she'd felt in the bookstore sent her pulse racing. She wanted to grab the front of his T-shirt and pull him up against her. Instead, she reached for one of the buckets.

Logan stepped to the side. "I've got this. If you don't mind walking through cow fields, I could use a hand running the hose out to the watering troughs near the barn. It will reach the first two enclosures."

He was sending her out to pasture. Alone. "I think I can handle that."

He nodded. "The hose is at the back of the barn. Half of the herd is in the first field, but they shouldn't bother you. The back one is empty at the moment. I'll be working in the front if you need help."

Logan turned and headed off. Sadie took that as her cue to start her chores. The sooner she finished, the sooner she could find him and ask for another task, one that required two people. Eventually she'd learn why he was so intent on pushing her away.

Two hours later, Sadie knew she'd found trouble. She'd filled the first two troughs easily enough. Then she'd spotted the third, smaller pen with tall metal fencing set apart from the others with one big cow pacing in circles. Figuring she would be doing Logan a favor, one he might thank her for later, she pulled the hose over and opened the metal gate.

Big mistake. The cow, or rather the bull—how had she missed the horns?—charged past her, knocking her off her feet. Her eyes widened in horror. She waited for the animal to run for the road. But, no, he headed straight for the pastures Sadie had just watered, and gracefully—which was flat-out astounding given his size—leaped over the lower wire fence.

"Shit, shit, shit!" She sprung to her feet and ran for the

barn. She needed to find Logan. Fast. And she had a sinking feeling this wouldn't make him laugh.

LOGAN HAD KNOWN he'd run into Sadie. She was living on his aunt's property. Part of him—the same part that reacted to the sight of her long legs in those shorts—had been eager to see her again. But common sense told him to stay away from the sexy, vibrant writer.

Ten paces back from the last empty water trough, Logan's phone vibrated in his pocket. Not many people had his number. It was probably Aunt Lou calling to harass him about the raffle.

Logan set the overflowing buckets down and retrieved his cell, glancing at the caller ID. Or his commanding officer calling him back to active duty.

"Colonel," he said.

"Reed," Lieutenant Colonel Walt Johnson barked. "How are you?"

He closed his eyes and pressed the bridge of his nose between his thumb and finger. "Fine, sir. Ready for duty."

"I'm not calling you back yet. You're to remain on R & R until we handle the fallout from your last mission," Johnson said. "I am in New York with Chief Cross. Your teammate will be working with the writer who is so damn intent on digging into your little joyride. Cross will act as her official liaison, helping her set up interviews with your team. Unofficially, he's under orders to control the message of her book."

"Sir, if there is anything I can do—"

"There is. Sit tight and stay the hell out of trouble. Don't talk to the press. I don't care if a kid wants to interview you for their fourth-grade paper. The answer is no. Do you understand?"

There was only one response to that question. "Yes, sir."

"Trust Chief Cross to do his job."

"I do." Logan's team was like family. They had each other's backs. Always. And Hunter Cross never failed when it came to a mission—or a woman. But if he messed this one up? Logan's career was likely over. The last thing the top brass wanted to see was *mistake* and *Special Forces* in the same sentence. Not to mention the fact that after publicity had rained down on the SEAL team who'd taken out bin Laden, the army wanted the Rangers to stay out of the media. Period.

"Expect a call in the next few weeks. When that call comes, be ready to return to work. Do whatever you need to do. Talk to a shrink if that is what it takes. The minute you set foot on base, I need you here and focused. One hundred percent. Are we clear?"

"Yes, sir."

The line went dead. Logan slipped his cell into his pocket and reached for his water buckets. It was almost over. In a few weeks, this clusterfuck would be behind him. All he had to do was make damn sure he had a handle on how to move forward with his life, how to be something more than the guy who'd lost his young wife to cancer. And while he worked on that, he had to keep a low profile, stay out of the media and away from writers.

Like the one living in his aunt's guesthouse and watering his cows. Didn't mean he couldn't daydream about Sadie's long legs, or—

"Logan! Logan!" The mental picture in his head, the one he'd been unable to stop replaying over and over since she'd walked up to him wearing those too-short shorts, carried a similar soundtrack, but without the panic.

"Logan!"

He dropped the filled buckets and ran toward the sound of Sadie's voice. She came racing around the corner, barreling straight into him. He pulled her close, preparing to take the brunt of the fall as they hit the ground. Stumbling back a step, he felt something hit the back of his knees, sending them both tumbling into a recently filled trough. She landed squarely on top of him, her long wet limbs tangling with his, rubbing back and forth as she flailed about in the water.

"Oh, God, I'm so sorry," she said.

The adrenaline rush combined with the feel of her body against his. The wet, frantic friction overloaded his senses. He could feel every inch of her wet limbs gliding over his. And it was too damn much.

Without a word, Logan dunked his head back and let it sink under the water, hoping to find some perspective. But the only thing waiting for him was wanting. It had been so long since he'd felt anything like it. The desire to strip away her shirt, to touch her, while she rode his thigh…

Christ, she'd knocked all the common sense out of him. He couldn't go there. Not with her. As far as threat levels went, she was more than a few notches above a fourth-grade reporter, even if he didn't know for sure if she was a journalist.

Slowly, he lifted his head. Sadie's wild thrashing had stopped. Her hands rested on the side of the tub, lifting her top half out of the trough. Her bottom half straddled his waist, a knee on either side of him, but she was doing her best to keep her body lifted off his.

"What happened?" he asked.

"I let the bull escape."

"You went into Titan's pen?" He looked her over, this time checking for signs of injury. "Are you okay?"

"I'm fine." She pressed down on the sides of the trough and lifted herself out. He missed the contact instantly. "But he jumped the wire fence."

Logan sighed. "And now he is in with the heifers."

"I'm sorry."

He stood, his soaking wet clothes forming a puddle in the dirt at his feet. "Not your fault. I should have warned you to steer clear of him."

She crossed her arms in front of her chest, obscuring his view of the tank top clinging to her like a second skin. He wasn't sure if he should be grateful or not.

"What do we do now?" she asked.

Logan looked out at the heifers' field. He had a list a mile long of the things he wanted to do, but he knew what needed to be done. "Round him up."

They spent the next hour chasing one very determined bull. Or rather, he chased the bull and Sadie did her best to distract him, running around in those damn shorts. Still, he had to give her credit. She put her heart into the chase, waving her arms, screaming at Titan. She looked so damn cute he half expected the animal to follow her home. Hell, he wanted to.

When they finally secured the bull in his pen, she turned to him. "Not how you planned to spend your afternoon?"

He let out a laugh. "No."

She smiled and it lit up her whole face. "Come back to the guesthouse with me. Those rocking chairs on the front porch are calling my name. And I owe you a cold drink."

He knew he should turn around and head back to his chores. Maybe change into dry clothes. His jeans and shirt were damp, though no longer dripping thanks to the hot afternoon sun. Still, clean clothes were probably a good idea. But after herding a bull, he was too tired to fight the attraction.

"All right," he said.

She led the way around the barn and up the three wooden steps he'd rebuilt when he'd first arrived back home. Waving toward the pair of green rocking chairs, she said, "Wait here and I'll grab our drinks. Beer, water or orange juice?"

"I'll take a beer."

Sadie disappeared through the front door and he settled into a rocker. Eventually, he'd get around to asking her what kind of writer she was. He hoped like hell her answer wouldn't be "reporter."

The door swung open and Sadie appeared carrying two bottles, a pair of forks and a pie dish. "I don't know about you, but I'm starving. And the only thing I have is half a leftover apple pie from The Quilted Quail."

"I like pie. Here, let me get that." Logan took the dish from her hands.

"Thanks." Sadie claimed the empty rocker, and handed him a beer and a fork. "Dig in."

They passed the dish back and forth in silence, sipping their drinks, and watching the sun sink lower behind the green mountains and casting long shadows over the cow pastures. It wouldn't be dark for several hours, but they were well into late afternoon. Aside from the occasional moo from the field, everything was quiet.

"I'm sorry again about letting Titan out," she said. "As you can probably tell, I don't have much experience with farm animals."

"Now you know to steer clear. Messing with a bull." He shook his head. "It's risky."

She laughed. And hearing that sound—it was worth spending an hour chasing a horny beast.

"You don't get anywhere without taking risks and looking for new adventures," she said.

Logan nodded slowly, digesting this bit of wisdom. "This is where you're looking to go? A rural Vermont cow farm?"

"If you'd asked me that a couple of days ago, I would have said absolutely not, I'm just here for my sister. But right now, I'm thinking I like it here. Risks and all." She turned to him. "What about you? Is this where you want to be?"

"I'm enjoying the company right now." He lifted his beer bottle to his lips, not meeting her intense gaze. The way she looked at him—it felt as if she could see straight through him.

"But?"

"Most days I'd rather be with my team than playing farmer," he admitted.

"Then why are you here?"

He shook his head. "Let's just say I screwed up. Big-time. That's why I'm home. I've been ordered to remain on R & R."

She raised an eyebrow. "You'd rather be at war?"

"It's what I do," he said. "Being in Mount Pleasant is driving me crazy."

"Ah, the raffle."

"That's part of it." There were also the memories, some good and some that reminded him of all the mistakes he'd made in his life.

"Are you going to do it?"

He watched as she licked her fork clean, her lips running over the utensil until she'd consumed every last drop. He'd never been attracted to the way a woman ate pie before. But everything about this woman's mouth turned him on. "Probably. Aunt Lou will insist."

"And you always listen to your aunt?"

He shrugged. "Most of the time."

"That's sweet." She smiled, piling another large bite onto her fork.

"My mom passed away when I was a kid and my dad,

well, he was never in the picture. My aunt and uncle raised me. My uncle died of a heart attack three years ago. Lou is… She's all I have left." He heard the grief in his voice and knew he should have kept his mouth shut.

Logan brought his beer to his lips and drained it, careful not to look over at Sadie. He wanted something from her, but not pity. Still, he felt her gaze on him, studying his profile. He had a feeling she wanted to ask him a question.

"Whatever it is, go ahead and spit it out."

She turned her fork over in her hands. "You said you screwed up. What happened?"

Logan looked off into the surrounding Green Mountains. Lined with evergreens, these peaks were a world away from the ragged war-ravaged cliffs in Afghanistan. He was about to feed her his automatic "that's classified" response, but first he had to know why she was digging. "Aunt Lou said you're a writer. Are you a reporter?"

He studied her face, waiting for her answer. But he knew before she opened her mouth that his paranoia had pushed him way off base. Her brow furrowed with surprise. Then laughter transformed her face, making her eyes sparkle.

"Nope," she said. "Not even close. I write fiction."

"All right, then," he said. "The answer to your question is classified. I can't talk about my missions."

"Fair enough," she said. "I'm going in for another. You want one?"

"I'm thinking about it," he said.

She cocked her head to one side and looked at him, her gaze burning a path down his body before she nodded and headed inside. He watched the screen door close behind her. If she could set him on fire by just looking at him, what would happen when he touched her? Did he want to find out?

Yes. No hesitation. It was the first time in months he'd made a split-second decision, one that felt certain and solid. After all, his colonel had told him to do whatever it took to move forward. He had a feeling going after Sadie, kissing her, maybe more, would do more for him than sitting down with a shrink. Logan stood and followed her inside.

SADIE HEADED DOWN the short hall, her mind still turning over his words. She'd been on the verge of asking him whether he was married, but something in his voice had stopped her. The depth of his grief when he talked about his family seemed too raw and fresh for a childhood loss. It left her wondering about his secrets again. Everyone had them, but his seemed edged with sorrow. And a far cry from a married man looking to sneak around on his wife.

She'd thought about offering the usual expression of sympathy, but she had a hunch this wasn't a man who wanted pity. She'd rather see him laughing, and maybe after another drink or two, naked.

She carried the empty bottles to the kitchen and found two more, setting them on the counter. Closing her eyes, she leaned back against the fridge. A picture of Logan without his work jeans and T-shirt filled her mind. She'd seen the outline of those muscles when she'd sent them both tumbling into the water trough. But her imagination went a step further, picturing him in the shower, wet and glistening, begging for her to touch and taste.

In her fantasy, he stood back against the wall, his hands flat on the tiles. It would take all of the man's willpower to keep his hands off her, but he would if he wanted to feel her mouth on him. She'd make that clear. And like a good soldier, he'd follow her orders.

The wooden floorboards creaked in the hall and Sadie opened her eyes. The erotic shower scene vanished, but it had left its mark. She was leaning against the fridge practically panting with desire, the downside to having an overactive imagination.

Logan turned the corner. She saw him hesitate for a second and guessed he'd noted her come-and-get-me look. He crossed the kitchen and planted one hand on either side of her head. Holding his body away from hers, he looked down into her eyes before dropping his gaze to her parted lips.

That look—it was part question, part warning. He wanted to kiss her. He planned on kissing her. And right here, right now, she wanted the real thing, no more almost-kisses in bookstores. But he didn't move.

"Kiss me," she demanded.

Heat flared in his eyes.

"Now," she added.

He lowered his head until their lips almost touched. And then, damn him, he froze.

Sadie reached out, grabbed his hips and drew him close, craving contact. This man wanted her. She could feel it. But something had a hold on him. And she needed to know what it was.

Running her hands up from his hips, over his oh-so-tempting chest and shoulders, she moved to his biceps, then down his powerful forearms to his hands. Entwining her fingers with his, she forced him to release his hold on the fridge.

"The other day, in the bookstore, you started to say something. You said 'I'm a'—but never finished the sentence. Now might be a good time to tell me."

5

LOGAN CLOSED HIS EYES. One kiss. That was all he wanted. One kiss before he watched pity eclipse her laughing, playful expression. Christ, she wanted it, too. The way she'd said that one word—*now*—had turned him inside out with need. But he'd hesitated, damn it.

"Logan?"

Opening his eyes, he stepped away, his arms falling to his sides. He didn't have a choice now. He had to tell her. "I haven't kissed a woman in a while."

She nodded, watching him, waiting for an explanation.

"It's been more than a year." Longer since he'd claimed a kiss that would lead to more. "I—"

A loud ring echoed in the kitchen.

Sadie's eyes widened. "The landline." She raced across the kitchen to the cordless phone on the far wall. "Hold that thought. I need to get this."

She frantically punched a button on the phone. "Laurel? Are you having the baby?"

Logan blinked. If the woman on the other end said yes, he needed to make himself scarce. Talking about his late wife while her sister was in labor? Not going to happen.

"Dinner?" Sadie closed her eyes. "I'm the worst sister in the world. I got caught up in something and forgot. Laurel, I'm so sorry. I'll be right there."

Sadie hung up the phone and turned to him. "I'm sorry. I completely lost track of time. I promised my sister I'd be back for dinner."

"No problem. I'll head out."

He shoved his hands in his pockets and headed for the door. Her sister had bought him some time, but he knew if he wanted to kiss this woman he had to tell her that he'd lost his wife to cancer. If she stuck around long enough, someone in town would volunteer the information.

But after he told her, would she order him to kiss her? Not likely. No matter how that conversation played out in his mind, it didn't lead to her mouth on his and her body tight against him.

"Logan?"

He paused in the archway between the kitchen and the hall. "Yeah?"

Sadie smiled, her expression still brimming with heat and laughter. That look—it made him want things he might not be ready to handle based on his performance today.

"If Laurel's still pregnant tomorrow," she said, "I could help you with the farm chores."

He raised an eyebrow. After he'd chickened out when she'd demanded a kiss, she was still interested? Part of him wanted to say, *Forget the chores, let's start again here. In front of the fridge.*

But this woman was trouble. Her laughter drew him in like a drug. He wanted to take her to bed. He wanted to talk to her and tell her things he hadn't shared in a long time—only he couldn't. He wasn't ready.

"I promise to stay away from Titan," she added.

The answer was no. He knew that, but— "I was planning to repair the heifers' birthing pen," he said. "I could use a hand. Come find me in the barn tomorrow morning."

"I'll bring the coffee."

SADIE RUSHED INTO her sister's cramped kitchen, letting the screen door slam behind her. Out of breath from running across the fields adjoining the two properties when the sun was so low behind the clouds she could barely see—this was why people drove cars short distances in the country, no streetlights!—Sadie stared at her sister.

"You didn't tell me Louise Reed had a ruggedly handsome nephew," she said.

Seated at the kitchen table beside her husband, Laurel looked up from her half-empty plate. "Are you late for dinner because you were with the supersexy soldier?"

Greg, her twin's husband, glanced up, a fork full of steak and potatoes suspended inches from his mouth.

"No." Sadie sank into the empty chair next to Laurel.

Her sister eyed her suspiciously. "Are you sure? If you were, I want details. Especially the naked ones."

Greg set his fork down on his plate and pushed back from the table. "That's my cue to leave."

"I was not *with* him. Not like that." But she'd thought about it.

"Yet," Laurel said.

Sadie waited until she heard Greg turn the TV on in the other room before she nodded. "Yet."

"He's an army ranger."

"I know," Sadie said.

Laurel smacked the wooden table with her open palm. "So you talked to him."

"I helped him with the farm chores. And afterward, I fed him pie."

Her twin's eyes sparkled. Leaning forward as far as

her belly would allow, she spoke in a low voice. "I heard a rumor he rode a horse into battle. And Cindy said—"

"I'm not interested in gossip," Sadie said, shaking her head. "If I want to know something, I'll ask him."

"You're planning to see him again?"

If she had her way, she'd do more than see him. But sharing her interest with Laurel didn't feel right. She was here to help her twin, not the handsome soldier who might have ridden a horse through a war zone. God, that sounded hot. Part cowboy, part soldier and all muscle—the man was a walking, talking fantasy. With secrets. She couldn't forget about those.

"I'm living in his aunt's guesthouse," Sadie said. "I'll probably bump into him again."

"So no plans?" Laurel pressed.

"I might have agreed to help him repair a birthing pen for the heifers," she admitted. The downside to not spending time with Laurel—she forgot how easily her twin knew when she was fudging the truth. "But only if you don't need my help."

Laurel raised an eyebrow. "You're going to fix a birthing pen? Did you tell him you don't know a screwdriver from a hammer?"

"He didn't ask. And I'm not that hopeless. Anymore."

"When was the last time you used either?"

Sadie picked at the potatoes on her plate. "Not recently."

"Yeah, you'll be a great help." Laurel stood and began clearing the table. "You're going to end up having wild sex in a barn while I sit here watching my feet swell."

Guilt came crashing down on her. Sadie abandoned the steak dinner she'd barely touched and brought her dish over to the sink to help her sister. "If you need me, I'm here."

Laurel waved her away, taking the dirty dish from her hands. "No. You should have sex with the soldier."

"I'm not looking for a vacation fling," she said. "You know that is not why I'm here."

Laurel placed the untouched steak on a cutting board and began slicing. "That doesn't mean you shouldn't seize the opportunity. Your last relationship ended in disaster three months ago. And I'm willing to bet you haven't had sex since then. Am I right?" Laurel stopped slicing and gave her a pointed look. "I'm right," her twin said. "Get the loaf of bread from the fridge, please."

Sadie did as she was told.

"A fling is just what you need," Laurel continued. "Just do yourself a favor and don't tell him you write erotica."

Sadie set the bread down beside the cutting board, her gaze fixed on the dark night outside the window. The memory of her last failed relationship still stung. She was over Kurt, but the way he'd run for the hills the moment he'd learned about her career, claiming it would damage his future political career? That hurt clung to her. So did the fact that he'd assumed his career ambitions trumped hers.

But deep down she'd always known her work would be a deal breaker. When she'd revealed her pen name, Kurt had focused on the graphic, sexual elements in her book. She'd explained that her writing was about a young woman learning to ask for what she wants in a relationship. But still he'd asked her to walk away from the publicity and all the opportunities that went with it.

And she'd said no.

Success was important to her. She did not want her children to grow up wearing shoes that were a size too small because she couldn't afford new ones. She would not let Laurel's baby grow up wanting.

But Kurt hadn't understood her drive. To him, revealing her identity equaled trouble, not book sales and a flush bank account that would provide for her family.

"He asked me if I was a reporter," Sadie said.

"Logan?"

She nodded.

"Then you have many, many more guesses before he reaches erotica writer." Laurel laid six slices of bread on the counter. She paused and looked right at Sadie. "This is your chance to have a fling with a man before you broadcast your secret identity to the world. Think about it. This time next month every man you meet will see you as the woman who wrote a bestselling erotica series."

Do you honestly want to walk down the street and have everyone look at you and think "that's the woman who writes about threesomes"?

Kurt's words ran through her mind like a highlight reel from her breakup. She knew others would make the same assumptions. And as much as she liked sex, she was a "one man, one woman" kind of girl.

"You're right. I'm not looking forward to starting every first date with the guy wondering if I'm into the same things as my characters," Sadie said, while Laurel turned her attention back to the sandwiches. "Okay, I might do it. If he's interested." And he was. She'd felt the proof when pressed up against him.

6

MIDDAY LIGHT POURED in the bedroom window as Sadie searched for her sneakers. They were her only pair of shoes suitable for farm chores. She finally found them buried at the bottom of her suitcase. While she was lacing them up, her cell vibrated on the floor beside her.

"Anne-Marie," Sadie greeted her publicist. "I hope you have good news."

"Good and not so good. Are you sitting down?" Anne-Marie demanded in her raspy smoker's voice that made her sound like an evil woman hunting Dalmatian puppies to make a coat.

Sadie glanced at the bedside clock. Eleven in the morning. She'd lost track of time when she'd sat down at her computer early that morning to write a few pages. She was already late, and pretty soon Logan would start wondering if she'd flaked on him.

"I'm sitting, but I don't have much time."

"Make time," Anne-Marie said. "My good news—it is huge."

A thrill ran through her. "Huge as in a movie deal?"

"Close. I just spoke with the producers over at *Today in America.* They want to reveal the woman behind MJ Lane on live TV during the prime-time slot the day your next book releases. In addition to the interview, they will do a piece on how you moved to New York City from Maryland to seek your fortune. How you struggled, working as a secretary by day and a waitress at night in order to support your father, who served our great nation. And how you used your precious spare time to write your first book." Anne-Marie paused. "Your father is a veteran, isn't he?"

"Yes." And he was going to hate this story. The entire world knowing he relied on his daughter to make ends meet? He might not speak to her for months. There was even a chance he'd refuse to cash her monthly check. "He served."

"Wonderful," Anne-Marie said. "After they talk about your backstory, they will bring you out for an interview. If we play our cards right, we'll announce a major motion picture deal for *Isabelle's Command.*"

"Yes! Yes! Yes!" Sadie cried.

"Before you get too excited, you should know that it is a pretty big *if* at the moment," Anne-Marie said. "The studio is backing away from the deal. They're nervous about turning another erotica book into a major motion picture. The casting for that *other* erotica film hasn't been easy."

"I don't want to lose this, Anne-Marie." Sadie wanted to see her work made into a movie. And she wanted to add the hundred-or-so thousand dollars from that deal to her growing safety net. "What if we can find a way to keep the press interested and talking about MJ Lane until the show airs?"

"Perhaps. If the studio feels that you're a big enough name to warrant the risk, it might work. How do you plan to do that without revealing your identity?"

"I'll think of something," Sadie promised.

"Think fast," Anne-Marie said. "We don't have much

time. Now, for this interview you need to look like MJ Lane from head to toe. Something hot and sexy."

"Don't worry, I'll start shopping online tonight."

"It needs to be perfect," her publicist insisted. "This is the big break we've been waiting for. We're sharing the morning show plans with all of the bookstore accounts and they're begging for more copies on day one."

The morning show, the movie deal—this would change everything. She'd made more money than she'd ever dreamed of from the first book's sales. But taking her career to the next level would solidify her savings. It wouldn't just start her niece's college savings account, it would fill it with some left over for graduate school.

The success, the financial stability—it was everything she'd wanted from her professional life. But while her publicist rambled on and on about the perfect outfit and if they should hire someone to do her makeup, Sadie's mind drifted.

What would Logan think if he knew? Would he look at her differently? Probably. She didn't want to find out. She liked the way he looked at her now, as if part of him wanted to run away, but the other part couldn't resist her. Not the bestselling erotica writer, but Sadie, the woman who loved apple pie and beer, who was struggling to be a good sister and who failed miserably when it came to farm chores.

But in a few weeks, after the morning show, Sadie Bannerman would be forever tied to her erotica-writing alter ego. She would never walk away from the publicity. But still, the thought was a little daunting. Only a few more weeks of anonymity. Maybe less, if the news leaked before her morning show appearance.

"How many people know that Sadie Bannerman is MJ Lane?"

"Only a handful at *Today in America,*" her publicist assured her. "And a few at the movie studio."

"That increases the chance of someone finding out earlier," Sadie said.

"It does," Anne-Marie agreed. "But aside from that one photographer who snapped a few shots of you entering your building months ago, the press isn't actively pursuing the story."

Not yet, but that had to change if she wanted to lock down that movie deal.

"Anne-Marie, you saw the pictures that photographer took, right?"

"Yes. They were garbage. Mostly shot from behind. When his editor called I told him I could not confirm or deny your identity because I couldn't see your face. We don't need to worry about him."

"But if someone, an unnamed source, confirmed that the woman in the pictures is MJ Lane, the paper would run them?"

"Probably. But they would have a difficult time connecting those pictures to Sadie Bannerman."

"Still, people would start talking and wondering again."

"That's not a bad idea. Release one or two pictures. Keep the mystery alive," Anne-Marie said. "Should I place the call?"

"No, I'll do it," Sadie said. "But not yet. I want to think this through first. I'll call you with my decision. I'm not sure I'm ready to alert the media just yet."

She had promised Laurel a month. She'd said she would be here when her niece arrived. To keep her promise, she had a feeling the media would have to wait. If she released that photograph and someone connected her to MJ Lane, the timetable for her big reveal would fast-forward. She might have to choose between morning show appearances for her career and being here for her sister—

Sadie shook her head. She didn't want to face that choice.

"I need to run, Anne-Marie. But promise me, no leaks. I want to control this story. I don't want to cut my time here short or lose that deal."

For once, she wanted it all—family and career. If she could just find a way to make that happen.

"I'll do my best," Anne-Marie said. "But think about making that call. It's a good idea."

"I will."

Sadie hung up and grabbed the bag of steak sandwiches Laurel had prepared the night before, hoping they would excuse her tardiness. Not that Logan needed her help. She probably would have been in the way.

When Sadie reached the barn, she opened the metal gate and searched for Logan. She found what she assumed was a newly constructed birthing pen, but no sign of the man responsible. Guessing he'd moved on to another task, she followed the fence line until she found him by the back pasture unraveling a spool of wire.

"I guess you didn't need my help after all," she said. "I stopped by the barn. The pen looks great."

Logan shrugged. "It would have gone faster with another set of hands, but I made do. I figured you got held up. How is your sister?"

"Still pregnant."

He set the wire down by the fence post. Reaching in his back pocket, he pulled out a handkerchief and wiped his brow. It was warm out today and his tanned skin glistened with perspiration. She couldn't help but notice how his white T-shirt clung to his muscles. Her gaze traveled down his body. Despite the heat, he wore jeans, and—oh my—were those cowboy boots?

Her sister's words from the night before ran through her mind. *I heard a rumor he rode a horse through Afghanistan.*

She would ask him about that, and more. Like why a year had passed since a man who looked like a movie star had kissed a woman. Maybe he'd been deployed for so long he hadn't had an opportunity?

"Want to give me a hand with the fences?" he asked, bringing her back to the present before her imagination ran wild with what-if scenarios.

"I have to be honest with you. I'm not great with tools," she said.

"All you have to do is hold the wire in place." He retrieved the spool. "I'm done with this stretch, but there is another section farther back that needs work."

"I think I can handle it." She held up the brown paper bag. "But what do you say we break for lunch first? Steak sandwiches courtesy of Laurel."

He returned the spool to the ground. "Sounds good. There's a nice spot on the other side of the trees to sit and eat. If you don't mind the hike."

His gaze traveled down over her legs to her feet. The jeans and running shoes she'd worn to help with the chores didn't exactly scream fun and sexy, not like his cowboy boots, but they seemed appropriate for the farm. He gave a nod and she assumed he agreed.

They walked side by side through the cleared grass to the tree line. Logan didn't say a word. He wasn't a big talker, she realized. He chose his words carefully. Unless he was relaxed and laughing like the other day at the bookstore. But she had a feeling that wasn't the norm for him.

Today, he looked as if he was walking into an interrogation. As if he knew he owed her an explanation, but would rather have a root canal. She wanted him at ease. Smiling and teasing her like he had in the romance/erotica section.

"I can't remember the last time I went hiking," she said.

"I imagine you walk plenty in the city."

"I do," she admitted. "But it's not the same. When I was little my dad would take us hiking and camping every summer. I loved it. So did Laurel. I think my dad did, too, though he always seemed a little sad he couldn't take us on more expensive trips. We would lie out under the stars and he'd tell us all about the places he'd seen. England, Africa, Germany, they all sounded so exotic.

"But as kids, we loved visiting campgrounds, swimming in lakes and looking for wildlife. The only place we ever begged him to take us was Disney World. I think my dad was kind of horrified that we would rather see Mickey Mouse than Europe. He loved to travel. His job took him all over the world before we were born and my mom passed away."

They'd entered the wooded area while she'd rambled. She'd been watching her steps, carefully avoiding cow patties in the field, but now she looked up at the tall trees. Their branches touched overhead and the leaves blocked her view of the clear blue sky. Her foot slipped and she lurched forward. A hand reached out and caught her arm, preventing her from falling to the ground.

"You all right?" Logan asked.

"Yes. Thanks." She glanced down at his hand, still firmly wrapped around her biceps. She drew her arm closer to her body and the back of his hand brushed against her breast.

If this was one of her books, he would draw her up against that hard wall of muscle she was aching to explore and kiss her. One kiss would lead to more and soon she'd be naked, her back up against a tree while he drove her wild.

But this wasn't fiction. They weren't here to explore her fantasies. He hadn't even kissed her yet. And even if he did decide to tell her what was holding him back, even if he finally claimed her mouth, they would not be having sex against a tree.

Sadie glanced at a cluster of evergreens. There was nothing sexy about bark cutting into her back. And without a blanket, the ground was not an option. He could be the most talented lover in the world and she would still be thinking about the things that might be crawling underneath her.

Logan released his hold on her arm. "Not much farther now."

Sadie nodded and followed him out of the trees into the clearing. A group of flat, smooth rocks sat in front of a small pond. The forest and the surrounding mountains might be wild, but this place was landscaped.

"Nice," she said, taking a seat next to Logan on one of the rocks.

"My uncle put this in years ago when he was thinking about selling a few acres. Thought it would make a nice home site. But then he changed his mind." Logan opened the bag and pulled out the sandwiches. He handed her one and again their fingers touched. "Your dad. You said he liked to travel. What did he do?"

"He's a marine. Retired now and living in Maryland, but still a marine."

Logan nodded, but didn't say anything.

"Actually, he left not long after my mom passed. He wanted to make sure we had a parent around. After he left the service he never had enough for plane tickets. We were just getting by."

And, okay, now she'd revealed more than she'd planned. Her potential vacation-fling did not need to know how hard her father had struggled to be everything to his girls and still make ends meet. But there was something about being with Logan, out here so far removed from her daily life, that put her at ease. Or maybe it was the way he listened, glancing over at her every so often.

"How long have you lived in New York City?" he asked.

"I went to college there. About eleven years." She took a bite of her sandwich, watching as he processed that information and determined her age. "Don't worry," she added. "I wasn't a child prodigy or anything. I'm not that young."

He smiled, but it didn't touch his eyes. He looked so damn serious. "I'm still older than you."

"And wiser?"

Logan shook his head. "I doubt that."

He set down his empty sandwich wrapper. The man ate as if it was a race. Or maybe he was used to having to eat and run? She'd never been to a war zone, but she could image there wasn't a lot of time to sit around and savor a meal.

"I'm sure you could teach me a thing or two," she said.

"About some things," he said, his voice low. "But I get the feeling you could broaden my horizons."

"Maybe." Seeing him in those cowboy boots, she wanted the opportunity. "But I'm still struggling with the no-whips thing. I think you should reconsider."

He laughed, shaking his head. "Yeah, I'm not so sure about that."

Finally, he'd relaxed. He didn't have that distant look in his eyes anymore. She watched as he drew his leg up, resting his foot on the rock. His boots were worn and dusty. They looked like they'd been to battle and back.

"It is true you rode a horse through Afghanistan?"

His laughter vanished and she wished she could take her question back. Better to keep him talking about kinky sex. Instead, she'd stuck her foot in her mouth and they were back to square one.

He studied her as if looking for some clue. "Sure you're not a reporter?"

"Not even close. Fiction only. I swear."

"I don't read much these days. I read the last Lee Child. Is that similar to what you write?"

"No. I've only published one book," she said, leaving out the international-bestseller part. "But it was a story about a young woman's journey to self-discovery. And you didn't answer my question."

"Yes, I did ride a horse on my last mission."

She pictured him mounted on a wild black stallion, his gun drawn as he raced into battle. That image—part Wild West, part Rambo—sent a shiver through her body. Of course, the reality was probably very different from the romantic version in her head. "Not going to tell me any more?"

"I can't talk about my missions."

"I can live with that. Just imagining you on a horse in your uniform? That's pretty sexy." She set her hand on his thigh. His muscles tensed beneath her touch. And that, more than any fanciful story she'd created about his top-secret mission, turned her on.

"Probably wouldn't think that if you'd been there. None of us knew how to ride and our horses looked like they should have been put out to pasture a decade before we arrived."

Sadie cocked her head to one side, pretending to reconsider. "Nope. Still sexy."

He looked at her, his brow furrowed. Then he turned away, shaking his head. "If you say so."

"I do." She moved her hand an inch up his leg. "Before I pin you to this rock and take advantage of you, cowboy, I think there was something you wanted to tell me."

Her hand stilled as she watched his expression transform, desire taking a backseat to something that looked an awful lot like regret. So much for trying to keep the mood light and playful. One look at him now and she'd never suspect this man had been joking moments earlier. He looked ready to face a firing squad.

But if he couldn't kiss her until he revealed his big secret, then she refused to let him off the hook now. She wanted a kiss from this cowboy soldier.

"Logan?"

He placed his hand over hers, keeping her fingers pressed against his leg. "I lost my wife. To cancer. About a year ago."

Her eyes widened. She should have asked Laurel for more information after all. This revelation? Not something she wanted taking her by surprise.

"I'm a widower."

7

LOGAN WATCHED AND waited for Sadie to shower him with condolences. He shouldn't have brought her out here. Not for this. Even if he carried her back to the barn, it was a five-minute walk. More like ten at her pace. Ten excruciating minutes of listening to the woman he wanted to kiss senseless offer her heartfelt sympathy.

Her fingers pressed into his thigh, giving a light squeeze. He glanced down at their hands, his still covering hers. She probably wanted to pull away, to break the physical connection. He lifted his hand, but hers didn't move.

"Logan?"

He looked up. She wasn't smiling and there was no laughter in her green eyes, but she didn't look sad.

"Do you have children?" she asked.

"No." That was the short answer. The long one—he wasn't interested in going down that road right now.

"That's good. I lost my mom when I was a baby. And… it's hard to raise kids on your own."

"Yeah," he said. "It would be. Especially with my job."

"Can I ask you something else?"

He nodded.

"Are you ready to move forward?" Her tone was quiet

and gentle, but not there was no trace of "oh, you poor, poor man." She wasn't making assumptions, he realized. She wanted honest answers.

"I need to," he said.

"You didn't answer my question. I've never met someone I wanted to spend the rest of my life with. I can imagine almost anything, but I can't imagine how it feels to lose that person so completely. Or how you feel."

Logan leaned his head back and closed his eyes. Everyone from his aunt to his teammates had offered pity and condolences. They wanted to know how he was doing, how he was coping with his grief. But no one had asked him how he felt. They'd all assumed they knew.

"For the first few months, it was like being submerged in water. At first, I wanted to sink to the bottom and drown." He opened his eyes and looked at her. "After a while, I started fighting to reach the surface. The grief still hits me. Hard sometimes. And often I feel so damn alone. But I don't want loneliness and grief to be the only things I feel anymore. Haven't wanted that for a while."

Sadie nodded. "So where are you now? Swimming to shore?"

Sitting here with her, he was so close to the shore he could practically touch it. "Something like that."

"And you're ready to look forward, not back?"

"Honestly? I'm not sure," he said. "I'd like to find out."

"Okay, then." Sadie slid off the rock, taking the empty lunch bags with her. "How about we finish fixing that fence and then head over to my place for a beer?"

"Sounds good." He looked into her eyes. They sparkled with anticipation and acceptance, no sign of pity. He hadn't lost her. Christ, he wanted to wrap his arms around her just for that gift. But not here. He'd wait until after they finished the fence before he took her in his arms and claimed that kiss. He wouldn't think twice. Not this time.

HOURS LATER, SADIE climbed the steps to Lou's guesthouse with Logan at her side. She had spent the better part of the afternoon destroying three lengths of wire before giving up and letting Logan fix the fence. Wire cutters were not her friend. Watching him work had given her time to admire the view—there was something dead sexy about a strong man bending steel wire with his bare hands—and think about what he'd told her.

Mr. Ruggedly Handsome had lost the love of his life. He hadn't put it quite like that but of course he'd loved her. A man didn't think about drowning in grief over a woman who didn't own his heart.

When he'd first said that word—*widower*—she'd mentally moved him out of the vacation-fling category. Too much baggage.

But the way he'd look at her, as if he expected her to turn tail and run, made her reconsider. He might not be ready to fall in love again, but a fling? Two failed attempts to kiss her said no, he wasn't ready to act on the sexual tension threatening to ignite every time they were together. But the more time she spent with him, talking to him, the more she suspected he'd held back because he needed her to know his story before they moved forward. Their relationship might have a definite end date, but she sensed that he wanted her to get to know him a little.

As far as her requirements for hopping into bed with a guy? The fact that he'd told her about losing his wife put him squarely in the good-heart category. And he'd proved in the bookstore he had a sense of humor.

Maybe they were perfect for each other. Neither one of them was relationship material. She could barely balance her career and her family. And he wasn't ready to put his heart out there again. That sounded perfect to her. But there was only one way to find out for sure.

Sadie paused, her hand on the front door to the guest-house. He stopped behind her, so close she could hear him breathing.

"If you're having second thoughts, I can go," Logan said quietly.

She turned to him, pressing her back up against the door. "Is that what you want?"

"No."

One word. No hesitation. Sadie smiled.

He stepped closer, their bodies practically touching now. "I want to be here," he said, his voice low. "I've been thinking about it all afternoon."

He lifted a hand and brushed a few stands of loose hair away from her eyes. He'd touched her face, but she felt it everywhere. It left her dying to melt into his arms.

She held back. She wanted him to make the first move. But he was crazy if he thought he could get this close again and walk away. She'd had her fill of almost-kisses. Right here, right now, up against the front door, she wanted the real thing. Reaching up, she ran her fingers through his hair, guiding his mouth closer.

"Kiss me," she demanded.

Logan groaned and the space between them vanished. He raised one hand, holding her head in place. His other hand reached for her hip, drawing her lower body firmly against his. And then, his lips touched hers.

He kissed her slowly as if savoring every sensation. Sadie arched up into him. Every hard muscle in his body pushed up against hers—including the one she was most interested in.

Her fingers held tight, urging him on. He obeyed, kissing her harder, deeper, as if he wanted to stay there all night, which was fine with her as long as they lost the clothes. Running her hands down his neck and over his chest, she reached for the hem of his T-shirt.

Logan pulled back, capturing her wrists in his hands. Breathing heavy, he looked down at her as if that one kiss had blown him away.

Oh, honey, there is so much more.

He took a step back, releasing her. But he didn't take his eyes off her.

"I guess this means you're staying," she said.

"I guess it does."

Sadie nodded. She wanted more, so much more of the ruggedly handsome soldier, but she didn't want to rush him. And she was having second thoughts about getting naked on the porch with the sun still peeking above the mountains and the air smelling heavily of cow.

Or maybe that was her? She'd spent the better part of the afternoon sitting in a field.

She reached behind her and turned the knob. Taking his hand, she led him inside. "Ready for that beer I promised you?"

"Sure."

She could still hear the desire in his voice. Sadie smiled. "Help yourself. I'm going to grab a quick shower first. Wash away the cow pasture smell."

"I should do the same." He released her hand and stepped back toward the door.

"Don't leave." If he walked out, she wasn't sure he'd come back. He'd start thinking about what he'd told her and he might change his mind. After that kiss, she wasn't going to let him escape.

"Sadie, if you're worried about smelling like the fields, trust me, I'm ten times worse."

Join me. The words were on the tip of her tongue. But no, he wasn't ready for that. Not yet.

"There are two showers," she said. "Take the one attached to the spare bedroom. And I'll meet you in the kitchen."

Before he had a chance to argue, she turned and ran for her bedroom. He better not leave. She'd waited for him to make the first move, claim the first kiss, but now that he had, she planned to seduce him. Drive him wild. She would make damn sure this was a fling neither one of them ever forgot.

LOGAN TIPPED HIS head back and let the cold water run down his face. He'd waited until he'd heard Sadie turn the shower off in the master bedroom before he'd started the other one. He'd had a hunch there wouldn't be enough hot water to go around and he'd been right. But he could use a cold rinse right about now.

He'd kissed her. In the moment, he'd felt so goddamn alive. All the noise in his head—his grief, the mistake he'd made on his last mission—it had all faded into the background. For a few precious moments, there had only been Sadie's hands, her mouth and her body.

He'd felt connected to another person for the first time in months. And he'd wanted to hold on to that feeling. But then she'd started pulling at his T-shirt and alarm bells had gone off in his head.

Sexy-as-hell Sadie wanted things he wasn't sure he could deliver. After that kiss, he had a hunch he could handle something physical, but nothing more.

From where he stood, Sadie was all bubbling energy, laughter and beauty. She was the first person to hear the word *widower* and not look at him like he was a lost puppy. But as much as he wanted her, he refused to hurt her. He had to tell her before they went any further that this thing between them couldn't go anywhere. He'd been honest in the bookstore. Sex, nothing more.

Logan turned off the water and reached for a towel. He dried off, then pulled on his jeans and shirt, leaving his briefs, socks and shoes in a pile inside the spare bedroom door before going to find Sadie. He hadn't been out of the game so long that he thought it was a good idea to seduce a woman in the same clothes he'd worn to rebuild a fence, but he didn't have a choice. He needed to talk to her and he wasn't about to do that naked.

Hearing the clink of bottles, he headed for the kitchen. Sadie stood by the fridge, a beer in each hand, wearing an oversize gray T-shirt that only just reached the smooth white skin of her bare-naked upper thighs—and nothing else. At least, not that he could see. She shifted her weight and the shirt rode up a half inch on her right leg, revealing a hint of black lace.

His mouth went dry. As far as signals went, this one was crystal clear. Sadie planned to move beyond kissing.

Logan dragged his gaze away from her legs. With her long red hair hanging down her back, she looked like she'd just rolled out of bed to raid the fridge. Across her chest, he read the word MARINE. The way the fabric moved, he suspected she'd ditched her bra. He wanted to touch and find out. But he had to wait. Talk to her. Even if it killed him.

She smiled. "How about that beer?"

Logan nodded, taking the bottle. Still eyeing her T-shirt, he said, "We need to talk."

"Look I know you're army, but until I do laundry, I'm stuck with my dad's old shirt."

She walked past him, through the archway and across the hall into the living room. Logan followed, unable to take his eyes off the way the T-shirt brushed against the back of her legs as she moved. Just knowing that shirt could ride up at any moment sent his body into ready-for-action mode.

He looked away, fighting for self-control. The living room held a pair of brown leather chairs and a leather couch. A round, low coffee table stood in the middle with a matching end table between the two chairs. The furniture was dated, but clean. Aunt Lou wouldn't have it any other way. On the floor lay a brown shag rug.

Sadie sat in the middle of the sofa, curling her long legs up under her. Logan chose the armchair across the table, knowing if he touched her skin he'd be toast.

"I wasn't talking about the shirt. I have nothing against the marines." He kept his gaze fixed on her, his fingers playing with the bottle. "I don't know how to say this without sounding like an ass."

She raised an eyebrow, but didn't say anything.

"I can handle something physical, but that's it."

"So just hot sex?"

"Yes." He waited for her to uncurl her bare legs and walk away.

She brought her beer to her lips and took a sip. "Okay."

It was a damn good thing self-control had been drilled into him during training or he would have pounced on her. "That works for you?"

Sadie smiled, her expression a tantalizing mix of sweetness, understanding and pure sin. "I'm not looking for a relationship."

This woman, with mile-long legs and a body that could take a man from zero to sixty in seconds, wanted to stay off the market? "Why not?"

"I tend to put everything I have into my career. Mostly

at the expense of my personal relationships. My work is important to me. Especially right now. I'm at a crossroads."

He nodded, not quite following her. But what did he know about writing novels about a girl's journey to self-discovery?

"Laurel also needs me. And so does my dad," she said, turning the beer bottle around in her hands as she spoke. "I don't have space in my life for a relationship, especially not after I return to the city. In a way, that makes us almost perfect for each other."

He could go to bed with her, laugh with her and then, when he finally got the call, return to active duty—this time with good memories instead of a boatload of grief. "Yeah. I guess it does."

Her brow furrowed. "Were you looking for another answer? If you wanted out, if this is too much for you, just say so."

He shook his head. He wanted this. Her. Now that he knew they were on the same page, that he wasn't leading her on, the only thing running through his head was *touch her, feel her, claim her.* The primal need had thrust him so far out of his comfort zone he could barely think straight.

Logan set his full beer on the small table between the chairs. The sight of Sadie in that shirt was intoxicating enough; he didn't need alcohol. Resting his elbows on his knees, he looked her straight in the eyes, watching and waiting. Knowing when to take action, it was part of his job. But it had been so long since he'd been in this situation, he wasn't sure of his next move.

Sadie leaned forward, setting her beer on the ground. Slowly, like a cat settling in for a nap, she rested her forearms on the couch and extended her legs behind her. She made a pillow for her head with her hands and rested her cheek, her gaze still fixed on him.

One quick glance told him as much, but he couldn't keep his eyes on her face. Not anymore. Her T-shirt had ridden up the back of her thighs, revealing her black lace panties. His jaw clenched, every muscle in his body ready and waiting for a go.

"After two days of farm chores, I think I need a massage," she said in the same light and playful tone he remembered from the bookstore.

This time, he didn't second-guess. He stood, crossing the rug in two steps. Keeping one foot on the ground, he placed his knee beside her thigh and straddled her legs, careful to keep his weight off her. But his erection strained against his jeans, desperate to touch her naked flesh.

Not yet. More than a year of celibacy was a helluva long time, but he'd take this slow if it killed him. He wanted to make it good for her. Not just to boost his ego, but because he needed to see her pleasure.

"Touch me," she said.

Leaning forward, Logan lowered his hands to her shoulders. Pressing his thumbs into her T-shirt, he began to rub her back, finding the knots by her shoulder blades and applying gentle pressure.

"Oh, my God, you're good," Sadie murmured. "I was hoping for a couple of half-assed attempts to massage my back before you moved south, but you're amazing. Please don't stop."

Logan laughed. "I'm not planning on stopping, but I am going to work my way down your back."

With his thumbs pressed against either side of her spine, he ran his hands down. His fingers traced the contours of her body. She was slim with gentle curves. She felt damn near perfect. Logan moved past her low back to where her T-shirt met her panties. He continued until he touched her upper thighs.

Beneath him, she gasped, her hips lifting slightly, pushing up into his hands. He squeezed gently, urging her to be still as his hands moved back up over her underwear, slipping beneath the hem of her T-shirt. Touching the smooth, bare skin of her lower back, he began to knead the sore muscles.

He was fully dressed and she hadn't even touched him yet, but he still had to mentally run through his parachute checklist to keep himself from exploding. She felt so good beneath him. Touching her, it made the rest of the world disappear.

Her muscles tensed beneath his hands as she pushed her upper body off the couch. Resting on her elbows, she looked over her shoulder. Her lips parted and he could feel the rise and fall of her chest tick up a beat.

"You're great with your hands," she said. "And I like what you're doing, but I want more. I want to feel your mouth on me."

Without a word, he withdrew his hands from beneath her shirt. He gently pressed her shoulders, coaxing her to lie flat again. Running his fingers through her long red hair, he brushed it aside. Resting one palm on either side of her waist, he leaned forward until his lips touched the base of her neck. He took his time, trailing kisses down over one shoulder, savoring the sweet taste of her smooth skin. Retracing his path, he ran his mouth over her neck, up to her ear.

He wanted her. Badly. He'd been semihard for hours. Touching her had pushed him perilously close to needing release soon. But he didn't want to rush her. He'd rather follow her lead and learn what turned her on, what pushed her over the edge.

"I haven't done this in a while," he admitted, his lips brushing her ear.

She looked over her shoulder, her eyes bright and excited. Her lips curved into a playful smile. "Follow my orders, soldier, and you'll be fine."

8

Heat flared in his eyes. She could feel the tension in his body as he hovered over her. He was pure muscle. Logan could overpower her in a heartbeat. But he was ready and willing to give her control. And that drove her wild. Her body ached with need.

"Lower," she said. "Touch me lower."

He shifted his weight, moving down the couch a little. She missed his mouth on her skin. But then his hands slipped under her lace boy-short panties and she forgot about his lips. She shifted beneath him, spreading her legs and offering access.

"Keep going," she commanded.

He obeyed, drawing her underwear down to the top of her thighs, and then running his hands up over her. Glancing over her shoulder, she watched as he took in the view, not once looking up at her face. His jaw clenched and she knew he wanted to take her further. She arched her lower back, giving him a glimpse of the wet, slick folds between her parted thighs.

"Touch me," she said.

He ran his fingers down between her legs, teasing her

entrance with soft strokes. Sadie closed her eyes. Without waiting for her to ask, he thrust one finger inside her.

"Yes." She pushed back against his hand, rocking her body. Shifting her hands over her head, she pressed her palms into the arm of the couch, offering more resistance.

"More," she said, no longer sure if she was giving orders or begging.

He added another finger, thrusting against her in a rhythm designed to drive her wild, hitting a place inside that pushed her so close. He rested his other hand on her low back, running it over her skin toward her thighs.

"Oh, God," she whispered, closing her eyes tight as the orgasm shook her body from head to toe. He stayed with her, slowly softening his touch before withdrawing his fingers and lifting his other hand off her body.

Through a pleasure-filled haze, Sadie rolled beneath him. She reached for him, pulling Logan against her until his hips pinned her to the couch. Drawing his mouth down to hers, she kissed him hard, her hands gliding down the sculpted planes of his back. She could feel the muscles working beneath his T-shirt.

There was so much tension in this man's body. And while she wanted to see every inch of him in action, working hard as he thrust into her, right now she wanted him to relax. She wanted to take him to that place where he lost all control and fell mindlessly into pleasure.

Breaking the kiss, Sadie touched her lips to his ear, her hands on his arms. "Your turn, soldier."

His biceps went from tense to rock-solid beneath her hands. Was he ready for more?

"Tell me if I'm pushing too far, too fast," she said softly.

He let out a low laugh that was almost a growl. "Whatever you have in mind, I think I can handle it."

She released his arm, running her hand down his chest

to where his erection was nestled between her bared thighs. Through the fabric of his jeans, she touched him, pressing her palm against the large, wide ridge.

"But not for long," he added.

She had a feeling she was going to like what she found beneath his clothes. Sadie moved her hand up and down, teasing them both.

"I'm going to enjoy touching you. Tasting you," she said. "I think it is time for you—"

A high-pitched ring interrupted. Her mind, filled with images of Logan without his clothes, quickly switched gears. Sadie sat up, forcing Logan to shift his weight off her. The ringing continued, drawing her attention to the kitchen.

"The land line." Sadie scrambled off the couch, pulling her underwear up as she raced to the kitchen. The ringing stopped. "Damn it."

But then it started again. She snatched the phone off the wall. "Hello?"

"Sadie?" Laurel said. "Sadie, I need you." Her twin sounded terrified.

Sadie's grip tightened on the phone. "What's wrong?"

"I'm having the baby. My water broke."

"Now? You're not due yet."

On the other end of the line, her twin started to cry. And from the sounds of it, this wasn't a few heartfelt tears. Laurel was weeping.

"I know," her twin managed through her hiccups and sobs. "It is too soon. And I'm scared. I want this baby. I want my little girl. But it is too soon."

Sadie opened her mouth to reassure her sister everything would be fine. Women had babies early all the time. But she couldn't find the words. What did she know about having a baby? Maybe four weeks early was too soon.

Her twin screamed and Sadie dropped the phone. Oh, God, what was happening to her sister? She quickly picked it up. She needed to get to Laurel. Help her.

"Sadie, are you there?" She heard Greg's voice as she held the receiver up to her ear.

"I'm here," she said, her voice shaking. "Is Laurel okay?"

"Meet us at the hospital. I'm taking her there now."

The line went dead.

No, this could not be happening. Her sister could not lose that baby. She would not let that happen. Not to Laurel.

She heard footsteps. Logan. In her panic, she'd forgotten about the man who'd made her come on the couch. She glanced over and caught Logan adjusting himself.

"I'm sorry. I know I owe you an orgasm. But I need to get to the hospital. Laurel is having her baby. Now." She scanned the kitchen counter and scooped up her purse and keys.

"I'll drive you."

"I'm fine," she said, tossing her keys into her purse. "I just need to get to her."

"Sadie, you're about to walk out of the house without your pants on and I'm guessing you don't know how to get to the hospital."

She glanced down at her bare legs. Her sister needed her. Now. And she was standing half-naked in the kitchen. "Pants. You're right. I need pants."

But her feet didn't move. Her mind was racing in a million different directions. She wasn't even sure she knew where to find her pants.

Logan took action. He disappeared, returning with the jeans she'd worn earlier and a pair of sandals in one hand. In the other, he held his shoes.

"I found these," he said, holding out her pants. "Put them on and we'll go."

She did as she was told and followed him to his truck. Seat belt on, she closed her eyes and silently begged every higher power she could think of to keep her sister and her niece safe.

"I'm sorry our night came to an abrupt end," she said as they turned onto the main road, heading away from the Mount Pleasant downtown. "But I'm glad you were here."

"Me, too."

"That you were here or sorry our night ended so quickly?" she asked.

"That I was here, Sadie." He slowed the truck and turned right onto a narrow dirt road.

"You're right. I never would have found my way." She squinted as she peered into the total darkness.

"I'm taking back roads. They're faster."

"Thank you." The need to rush sent all the potential outcomes racing through her mind. What if there was something wrong with the baby? Or Laurel?

Sadie closed her eyes. She wanted to call Greg and demand answers, but she knew he was busy caring for her twin. The fear and worry threatened to overwhelm her and she refused to show up at the hospital a crying mess—not when Laurel needed her.

She opened her eyes. Up ahead, she spotted a lit sign announcing the hospital's emergency entrance. Logan bypassed the E.R. and turned in to the second parking lot. He pulled up to the front of the building, but kept the engine running.

"There's a receptionist inside," he said. "She'll direct you to the Labor and Delivery floor. I'm going to park and then I'll meet you there."

"Logan, you don't have to stay."

He smiled gently. "I don't have any other plans. I'll be here if you need me."

One hand on the door, she leaned over and kissed his cheek. "Thank you. Now I really owe you."

He laughed, shaking his head. "Go on, Sadie. Help your sister."

HOURS LATER, AS the sun was starting to rise, Sadie stood beside her sister's hospital bed, staring down at her newborn niece. Lacey. The baby was small, only five pounds, but perfect. And her twin had finally stopped crying.

When Sadie arrived, she'd found her sister screaming in pain, begging the nurses to keep her baby alive. An hour later, Laurel was threatening them with bodily harm if they didn't make the pain stop. Watching her sister scream like she was being tortured had turned Sadie into a pit bull—according to Greg, who'd remained strangely calm. She'd snarled and snapped at the nurses, vowing to find the anesthesiologist herself if he did not show up soon. The nurses had ignored her—and Laurel—proceeding to go about their jobs as if they saw women behave like this every day. In hindsight, Sadie realized they probably did.

But now, even after they'd helped bring her niece safely into the world, Sadie didn't feel the least bit sorry for the way she'd acted. Laurel had needed her help and she'd been there for her twin. For the first time, she'd felt entirely in tune with her sister's needs. The one-way communication that always seemed to flow from Sadie to Laurel but never vice versa had changed directions for a few hours.

Laurel took her hand and squeezed. "You were amazing tonight. I felt like we were six years old and trying to fight a team of dragons."

The nurse checking Laurel's IV raised an eyebrow.

Sadie leaned closer to her sister. "I don't think they appreciate being compared to mythical fire-breathing creatures."

Laurel laughed and the baby in her arms opened her eyes for a second before settling back into sleep. "I don't care what they think. You were my hero tonight."

Sadie fought back tears. She never cried. But hearing her sister's words? Her heart swelled. "You're welcome."

"I told the gentleman pacing in the waiting area both baby and mom were healthy," the dragon-nurse said. She looked pointedly at Sadie. "He said to tell you he would see you later." She turned and headed for the door.

Laurel's brow furrowed. "What man?"

"Logan. I can't believe he stayed. He was with me when you called. He drove me over here," Sadie explained quickly.

"You listened," Laurel said smugly. "You're having sex with the soldier."

"No, I was here with you, fighting dragons," she said.

"But you're going to."

"Maybe." She thought about the impressive erection she'd felt through his jeans. "Probably. But I don't know. He is a widower."

"He told you?"

Sadie gave her pointed look. "He did. The question is why didn't you mention it?"

Laurel shrugged. "You said no gossip."

"That's not gossip. It's a fact. A pretty important one."

"I wanted you to give him a chance," Laurel said. "Jane's been gone a long time."

"A year."

"She was sick for a while before that. And Logan's a faithful guy."

"So you're looking out for his sexual needs now?" Sadie didn't bother to hide her sarcasm.

"He's the hometown hero, and this is my home now," she said. "My family's home."

The newborn in Laurel's arms woke and started fussing, demanding attention. Greg returned a minute later with a selection of Laurel's favorite candy bars. Sadie decided it was time for her to leave and give the family some space.

She walked out of the main entrance and stared at the parking lot. She didn't have a car. She pulled out her cell and turned it on. The screen alerted her to a handful of missed calls from her father. She had to call him back and tell him about the baby.

"Dad?" she said when the ringing stopped.

On the other end of the line, her father launched into questions. Sadie answered them, feeling as if she was reliving the birth, minute by minute. While they talked, she found a seat on a metal bench. She thought about lying down and closing her eyes. It was tempting.

"And Laurel? She's all right?"

"She's fine," Sadie said for what felt like the third time in ten minutes. "Dad, I sent you extra money last month. Buy a ticket. Come up here. See for yourself."

Silence. If he didn't say something soon, Sadie suspected she'd fall asleep. "Dad, are you still there?"

"I already owe you more than I can pay back."

Sadie sighed. "It's a gift, not a loan. All of it."

"I can't take that much from you." She heard the familiar stubborn edge in her father's voice.

Sadie closed her eyes. Why was this so hard? A sane person with limited income would welcome a check for thousands of dollars. "Please, Daddy. For Laurel. She wants you here. I know she does."

"I'll think about it. I'd like to meet my granddaughter." There was a softness in his voice that she hadn't heard in a long time. It reminded her of bedtime stories and lullabies.

"But I'd miss work," he added. "I agreed to cover for my buddy at the hardware store next week."

She wanted to scream into the phone, *I'll pay you double, triple what you'd make at the store.* But that would only wound his pride and expand the gulf between them. And it certainly wouldn't get him on a plane.

"Some things are just plain worth it," she said.

There was another long silence.

"You're right."

Of course, she was right. She'd learned that lesson from him. He'd given up everything he'd wanted for himself, including his career, for her and Laurel. And he'd made it clear every day that they were worth it. Why couldn't he let her help him now?

"I'll think about it."

"Good. I'll send you pictures. I promise."

She ended the call and closed her eyes. She needed a nap; staying up all night, fighting dragon-nurses, it was exhausting. Her dad hadn't helped. She loved the man, but talking to him took every last bit of energy she had. Pulling her legs up, she rested her head on her arms. She'd lie here. Just for a minute.

"Looks like we should get you to bed."

Sadie opened her eyes. She wanted to hear those words from Logan's lips, but not when she was too tired to invite him to join her. And now he'd caught her passed out and drooling on her arm.

"Need a ride?" Logan asked mildly.

She sat upright and pushed off the bench. "Yes. And bed." She eyed the coffee cup in his hand. "You didn't have to wait."

He shrugged. "I left and grabbed a bite to eat at home. Then realized you didn't have a way to get back to the farm. Hard to catch a cab up here."

She followed him into the lot. "Your coffee. What do I have to do to—"

"It's yours." He handed her the cup.

"Thanks." Sadie took it, lifting it to her lips. Light and sweet. Perfect. "Now I owe you a coffee and an orgasm."

Logan opened the door to his truck, shaking his head. "I'm still wondering what you were going to offer in exchange for the caffeine."

She buckled herself in as he walked around the truck to the driver's seat. "Anything."

"I'll keep that in mind."

They drove in silence down the country roads. She might have closed her eyes for a minute or two. And then they were at her front door, the truck in Park.

"Need help getting inside?"

"I can manage." If she hadn't been up all night with Laurel, she would have asked him in and finished what they'd started. She released her belt and climbed out of the cab. She felt her phone buzz in her pocket and pulled it out. A text from Laurel.

We need a car seat. Planned to borrow one from a friend, but she is still using it. Can't bring the baby home without one.

"Everything okay?" Logan asked.

Sadie nodded. "Nothing that can't be fixed with a little online shopping and overnight delivery."

Still holding the truck door open, she turned back to face him. "Are you going to the festival tonight?"

He nodded. "No choice. My aunt cornered me and I agreed to the raffle. With one stipulation."

"The winner foots the bill for lunch?"

He laughed. "No. That I don't have to go up on stage.

I'll be there and I'll greet the winner afterward to set up the lunch, but that's it."

"Stage fright?"

"Let's just say I'm not comfortable standing up in front of a crowd," he said.

"Then I'll see you tonight. Maybe I'll be the lucky winner. I wouldn't mind lunch with the local hero."

He smiled. "If you are, I'll upgrade the prize from lunch to dinner."

"A real date? I thought we were keeping this casual." A date was one step away from relationship territory. Dinner dates and long meaningful talks about the future—those were off the table.

"We are. But if you save me from lunch with one of Mount Pleasant's single women, I'm buying you dinner."

Sadie had never been the jealous type, but she had a competitive streak a mile long. She couldn't win with her father, but taking on the women of Mount Pleasant?

"You're on."

9

IT WAS LATE AFTERNOON, the sun still high above the Green Mountains, when Sadie arrived at the Summer Festival. People milled about Main Street, which had been closed to traffic. Some perused the tables set up by local businesses while others made their way to the tented food area by the stage. Her stomach grumbling, Sadie headed for the food, pausing to let a group of kids, mostly preteens if she had to guess, cross the road, each one leading a goat or sheep.

"They're headed to the 4-H tent set up on the other side of city hall," a blonde woman said. "Getting them ready for the parade. The llamas and the cows should already be over there. Anyone who showed an animal at the county fair two weeks ago is invited to march."

"Oh," she said. What else was there to say about goats marching through town? Sadie turned to the woman who'd appeared at her side, unsure if she should be grateful the cloud of perfume surrounding the blonde had overpowered the farm animal smell.

"I'm Cindy. And you must be Laurel's sister."

"Sadie. How did you know?"

"You have the wide-eyed look of someone who has

never seen farm animals in town," Cindy said. "I heard about the baby. Congratulations!"

The perfumed stranger wrapped her arms around Sadie and gave her a quick squeeze before stepping back. "I hope you'll consider entering our raffle."

"I was on my way to purchase tickets." After food, she thought, but she could take a quick detour. "Where do I go?"

"Heading there myself. I'll take you." Cindy linked her arm through Sadie's and started walking.

Sadie did her best to keep up, already regretting the strappy high-heeled sandals she'd chosen to wear with her fitted sundress. She might as well have pasted a sign on her back that read Not From Here. Most of the locals wore jeans and boots or sandals that bore a closer resemblance to flip-flops than high heels.

When they reached the raffle table, Cindy released her and slipped behind the table. A teenager, slightly older than the kids with the goats but still in braces, stood beside Cindy.

"Tickets are a dollar each and all the money goes to the school's literacy program," Cindy said. "How many would you like?"

"Five hundred?"

Cindy's smile faltered and her eyes widened.

"I'm a big fan of literacy."

"Or she's met Logan," the teen said.

"That is very generous of you." Cindy had recovered her smile. "Certainly improves your chances. Cash or check?"

"Check." Sadie withdrew her checkbook from her purse. "When is the drawing?"

"Seven tonight. Please make the check out to the Mount Pleasant Literacy Fund." Cindy picked up a spool of tickets and began tearing. "Each side has a number printed on it.

One goes in the bucket and you keep the other. We'll select the winner before the band starts."

"The Wild Bucks are playing tonight," the teen supplied, as if Sadie should know the name. "They're from Boston."

"I'm from New York."

"I know," the teen said. "Everyone in town knows who you are."

Sadie froze. No. It wasn't possible. Aside from her family, her ex, a handful of people at her publisher and the group at the morning show, no one knew. Not yet.

"You're Laurel's twin," the teen continued. "The one living at Aunt Lou's. With Logan."

Relief hit her fast and fierce. Her secret was safe. But soon, it wouldn't be a secret. In a few weeks, she wouldn't be identified as Laurel's twin. Everyone she met would look at her and see MJ Lane, erotica writer.

"Annie," Cindy said, her voice filled with warning as she continued to tear tickets.

"What? It explains why she bought so many tickets."

It did, but Sadie wasn't about to advertise that fact to Mount Pleasant's under-eighteen set.

Annie stopped tearing and looked up at Sadie. "Jane, Logan's wife, was my third-grade teacher. I was in her last class before she switched to teaching special-needs kindergarteners."

"Annie, that's enough," Cindy said, tearing faster and faster. She was probably worried Sadie would change her mind about the five hundred tickets now that she knew Jane, Logan's late wife, had been vying for sainthood. Another detail her twin could have mentioned.

"She sounds lovely," Sadie said. "I'm sure you miss her."

Cindy quickly finished tearing and held out the tickets. "Here you go. Thank you so much for supporting our raffle."

"This town has welcomed me with open arms. I'm just happy to have a way to give back."

Judging from the looks on their faces, neither Cindy nor Annie believed her. Sadie gathered her tickets, stuffed them in her purse and fled to the food stand before the teen said another word about Logan's late wife.

Holding a corn dog on a stick, Sadie wandered the festival hoping to run into Logan. No such luck. But she watched the 4-H kids march down Main Street with their farm animals. *Parade* was not the word she'd use for the chaos created by kids leading goats down the street. The animals stopped to chew and explore everything. If it hadn't been for the older kids bringing up the rear with the cows, they'd all probably still be there. But at seven, the crowd migrated to the stage for the raffle and Sadie followed.

The stage consisted of raised platforms. Two large lighting booms stood on either side and there were a number of speakers on stands. A wooden dance floor extended in front of the stage. Long rectangular tables, each decorated with their own theme, were scattered about the street behind the dance floor.

Hoisting her overflowing purse onto her shoulder, Sadie found a place for the big announcement. If they called one of her numbers, it might take her all night to find the matching ticket. But she liked her odds of winning a date with Logan. And standing on the dance floor surrounded by women, she felt better about her investment.

Cindy took the stage, mic in hand. Two teenage boys wearing T-shirts that read Stage Crew Mount Pleasant High Drama Department followed Cindy. Between them, they carried a large wooden container built like a book.

Sadie would bet her raffle tickets the boys had helped build the bin. Everything about the Summer Festival lacked professional polish, but there was something downright sweet about how everyone in town contributed.

Part of her understood why her sister liked living here. Family had always come first for Laurel. And here, the community was like one giant extended family. There weren't a lot of jobs, certainly not high-paying ones, but everyone got by.

For Sadie, just getting by would never be enough. But her success came at a high price. Her relationships suffered. And soon, her career would strip away her anonymity, too.

But not today. She was still Sadie, Laurel's sister, hoping to win a date with a handsome soldier at the town festival.

"Welcome to Summer Festival!" Cindy's voice boomed through the PA system, echoing against the buildings that lined Main Street. "I hope you all brought your dancing shoes. Tonight, all the way from Boston, we have The Wild Bucks performing. Some of you might remember the lead singer, Trey Smith, a recent graduate of Mount Pleasant High!"

The crowd roared their approval.

"But before Trey takes the stage, we need to pick our raffle winner! The lucky ticket holder will win lunch with our local hero, U.S. Army Ranger Logan Reed. Aren't we fortunate to have him home safe and sound on leave for our festival this year? Logan, raise your hand."

Again the crowd screamed and cheered, turning their attention to Logan, who stood off to the right side of the stage. He'd dressed for the occasion in jeans and a white button-down shirt, the sleeves rolled up to reveal his forearms. She couldn't see his feet, but Sadie guessed he'd worn his cowboy boots. And she had a feeling she wasn't the only woman in the crowd picturing what he looked like without the clothes.

He raised his hand, but judging from the expression on his face, he wasn't thrilled by the reception. Or maybe he was trying to keep up the "stage fright" excuse, knowing if he didn't, Cindy would drag him up on stage.

"Before I reach into the book bin built by the high school drama club, I wanted to give you the final dollar amount raised," Cindy continued. "This year, we made a record seven hundred and fifty-three dollars!"

Another thunderous shout of approval from the group gathered by the stage, which, Sadie noted, had seemingly doubled since Cindy had started talking. Men, women and children of all ages gathered around.

"Now for the drawing. I've asked Mrs. Gracel, our school librarian, to do the honors." A young woman, probably close to Sadie's age, climbed the makeshift stairs to the bin. Smiling at the audience, she closed her eyes and made a show of reaching her hand inside.

Only a few seconds passed before Mrs. Gracel handed over the chosen ticket, but it felt like forever. Probably because Sadie had forgotten to breathe. She wanted to win. Badly.

"And the winner is…ticket number 5218!"

The crowd fell silent while everyone checked their tickets. Sadie opened her bag, silently cursing Cindy and the raffle organizers for not issuing tickets numbered one through seven hundred and fifty-three.

"I won," a high-pitched, clear voice announced.

Sadie looked up from her bag, expecting to see an eager young woman running to claim her prize—Logan.

Instead, a child who looked to be about ten quietly made her way through the crowd. The audience applauded, but the girl offered no sign of excitement. She simply walked up on stage and handed her ticket to Cindy.

"Congratulations, Charlotte!" Cindy said into the mic. She pointed off the other side of the stage. "He's waiting for you right over there. Go claim your prize."

She watched Charlotte march off the stage, still no signs of a smile. But even from a distance she could see the girl's hands trembling slightly. Poor thing was probably nervous. Sadie shook her head. Logan had been so worried about the single women trying to cozy up to him, he'd forgotten about the people who saw him for what he was—a living, breathing hero.

LOGAN HAD SURVIVED the raffle. But he still had to face the winner. Judging from the grim expression on ten-year-old Charlotte Matthews's face, she was on a mission. Logan had followed an Afghan warlord into battle, a man he wasn't sure he could trust, while riding a horse for the first time, and he'd never flinched. But watching Charlotte march over to him, he felt a stab of panic. What if she was writing an article for her fourth-grade paper about his latest mission?

He'd gone to school with Charlotte's mother. She'd been on the cheerleading squad with Jane. How was he going to get through lunch if he refused to answer the kid's questions? Christ, just thinking about it made him feel like a jerk.

"Mr. Reed." Charlotte stood in front of him, her hand extended.

Logan shook her small hand. "You can call me Logan."

The little girl nodded solemnly and looked him straight in the eye. "Did you know my dad? He was a hero. Like you."

Logan heard that one word—*was*—and he remembered. Charlotte Matthews's father had died last year. Right around the same time Jane had passed away. He'd been hit by an IED while on patrol in Afghanistan. Before he'd bled out from his injuries, he'd pulled three men to safety. The man defined *hero*.

Standing in front of his little girl, Logan felt like a fraud. "I did."

Charlotte nodded. "Did you work with him?"

"No. We served in different parts of the army."

"Oh."

That one word held a world of disappointment. This child had been hoping to learn more about her dad. She didn't want to write about him or expose his failures. She craved a connection to someone she'd loved and lost. For months after Jane's death, Logan had wanted the same thing.

But he was a grown man. And he'd lost his wife slowly to illness. A foreign war fought in a place Charlotte had never seen had claimed her father's life. A war her father had entered willingly. That had to be a hard thing to understand, doubly so for a child.

"I'm sorry, Charlotte." Logan knelt down on one knee so that he could look her in the eye. "You didn't need to enter the raffle to ask me about your dad. I can ask Cindy for your dollar back."

"No. I won," she said stubbornly. "I want to go to lunch."

If winning meant something to her, he wouldn't be the one to take that away. He'd take her to lunch and answer her questions. He'd feel like an impostor trying to fill the shoes of the war hero Charlotte wanted to see, but he would not disappoint her.

"When do you go back?" she asked.

"I don't know yet. Could be anytime. If you're free tomorrow, I can meet you in town at noon. If that's okay with your mom." He saw a hint of relief in her blue eyes. "We can go anywhere you want."

Charlotte nodded. "I'll meet you in front of Abagail's. Noon tomorrow."

Logan nodded. "I'll call your mom tonight to confirm, okay?"

He stood and watched Charlotte disappear into the crowd. Out of the corner of his eye, he spotted Sadie waiting patiently out of earshot. But as soon as Charlotte walked away, she came over.

The fabric of her sundress shifted around her legs, drawing attention to her smooth thighs. One look and he remembered what it felt like to run his hands over her skin. Logan welcomed the distraction, knowing he wasn't in the mood to act on it.

She'd lost the raffle, but that didn't change the fact that he was going to take her out on a date. He enjoyed her company, plain and simple. He'd never met a woman who could sit quietly while he repaired a fence, seemingly unconcerned by the silence. She drew out his secrets and still accepted him—wanted him.

She stopped by his side. "Sorry, I did my best." Sadie held up her ticket-filled purse as evidence and Logan chuckled.

"Look on the bright side," she said. "Charlotte probably won't consider lunch with you a 'date.' She looks like a sensible girl. I'm sure she knows she is too young for you."

"I don't know about that. She talked me into having lunch at Abagail's ice cream parlor tomorrow." He rubbed the back of his neck with one hand. "I think I would have preferred a real date."

"I'm still game for dinner."

Another woman would have tried to find out why one

little girl disturbed him. But not Sadie. She kept things light. He appreciated that she didn't press him—more than she could imagine.

"Good thing," he said, trying to match her playful tone and failing. "I made plans for tomorrow night."

He heard someone call his name and knew it was time to clear the area. He couldn't handle small talk. Not tonight.

Shoving his hands in his pockets, Logan turned and started walking away from the stage toward the roadblocks at the edge of Main Street. A number of people looked ready to approach him, but he picked up the pace and kept his head down. He'd done his part, letting them raffle him off, and look where it had landed him.

Sadie fell in beside him, linking her arm through his. "Where are we going?"

"Hadn't given it much thought."

"How about we circle back, sticking to the roads running parallel to Main Street? I'll run in and grab a couple of beers and cotton candy." Steering him with her arm, she led him down a side street. "The B and B in town has a balcony on the second story. What do you say we sneak in and watch the festival from up there?"

"Sure you don't want to dance? Enjoy yourself?"

She shook her head. "When I was a kid, I loved watching the world move around me. I would go to the playground, find the highest perch and watch the kids play. I think it is part of the reason why New York City works for me. There are so many places to sit and observe people."

Her plan—beer, junk food and a quiet place—sounded a helluva lot better than his. He'd thought he would walk until the festival started to wind down and then head back to his truck.

"I could go for a beer," he said. "But let's skip the inn.

Too crowded with folks visiting for the festival. Town hall should be open and I know how to access the roof."

It was like the bookstore all over again, the way they were embarking on a "mission" to escape the world. He watched her disappear into the festival crowd. Sadie. She bubbled with laughter and fun—when he needed it most.

10

SADIE PEERED OVER the brick wall on the top of Mount Pleasant's town hall. The sun had dipped behind the Green Mountains in the distance, but street lamps illuminated the people milling about Main Street, checking out the vendors' booths. The stage stood at the opposite end of the street from city hall. She could feel the bass, but not much else. Judging from what little sound drifted their way, she wasn't missing much.

"Nice view," she said. She'd come to the festival ready and willing to finish what they'd started last night before her sister had gone into labor. But now, she wasn't so sure. It felt as if he'd back-stepped to before he'd told her about his late wife. He seemed untouchable again.

"Look," Sadie said, pointing to the cotton candy booth. "There's your ice cream date."

Standing so close their arms touched, Sadie could feel the tension ripple through Logan's body. He held his plastic beer cup to his lips, but didn't drink. Something about the little girl bothered him. Sadie hadn't pressed him earlier, not in the crowd. But up here, where no one could interrupt them, it seemed like as good a time as any to ask. "Why does she frighten you?"

Logan lowered his beer. "Charlotte doesn't scare me."

"You can pretend to be the big, bad soldier all you want, but I think you're lying," she said. "I saw your deer-in-the-headlights look when she walked up to you."

She waited for a laugh, the beginning of a smile—nothing.

"At first I thought she might want to interview me for the school paper," he finally admitted, lifting the plastic cup to his lips again.

"Are you serious? You were afraid that little girl was a reporter?" she said.

"At first. But she's not."

Sadie set down her empty beer cup and crossed her arms over her chest. "Reporters and school children. These sound like irrational fears for a soldier who rode a horse against the Taliban, don't you think?"

Logan stared into his beer. "That mission. The one we completed on horseback. I screwed that one up. Big-time."

Pain and anger lined his face. Whatever had happened over there, he was holding tight to the blame. Maybe he deserved it and maybe he didn't. Either way, Sadie knew from experience that walking through life saddled with self-doubt wasn't easy.

"What happened?" she asked.

Time slipped by. She heard the crowd watching the band cheer as the musicians finished a song. A child screamed, begging for another cookie. And a cow mooed.

"You can't repeat this to anyone," Logan said.

Sadie rested her hand on his arm. There was something wild and hot burning between them, but this touch? It was pure comfort.

"Logan, you can trust me."

He closed his eyes, and for a moment, Sadie feared he wasn't going to say another word.

"We were on a rescue mission." Logan opened his eyes and stared down at the festival. "During the extraction, we came under fire. I was covering Hunter, one of my team-mates, but then…"

His hand tightened around his empty beer cup, break-ing the plastic. Was he back there? Sadie wondered. Reliv-ing the mission? What if his grief for his late wife wasn't his only baggage? What if Logan suffered from PTSD?

"I got distracted," he continued, forcing her to listen to his words, instead of letting her imagination run wild with what-if scenarios. "And Hunter got shot in the shoulder."

"Oh, no. Logan. I'm so sorry. Did he make it?"

He nodded. "He's fine. On a mission right now in New York to keep my mistake out of the press. Some profes-sor wants to write a book about what we did. He took a bullet because I didn't have my head on straight, and now he is having to clean up the mess, too, while I sit up here and wait."

"You want to go back." It wasn't a question. She hadn't known him long, but she knew he was a soldier through and through.

"Yeah. But I can't. Not yet. I've been ordered to stay here and keep a low profile. That means no reporters. Not even kids writing for school papers. No questions and nothing in print. If I can do that, I can go back to serving my country."

A familiar sensation washed over Sadie. Guilt. It was as if she smuggled that sinking feeling into every single one of her relationships. If she launched the who-is-MJ-Lane media circus that she needed to secure her movie deal, re-porters would start digging. There was always the chance they would find her here. If they found her with Logan, they might identify him and ask questions about why he was on leave. They could find out about his mistake. Based on what he was telling her, if that happened, she could damage his chances of returning to the job he loved.

If someone did that to her…

Sadie pushed the thought away. Right now no one knew. And a half-dozen *if*s stood between her connection to Logan and the possibility that the media would delve into Logan's missions. By the time she went on national television, their fling would be over. She would be back in New York and he would be God knows where doing the job he loved.

And she would make certain no one ever linked him to her. Ever.

"That explains your dread of reporters," she said, forcing a light, playful tone. "But not your fear of little kids. Are you worried her mother will report you for feeding her daughter ice cream for lunch?"

"Charlotte thinks I'm a hero," he said quietly. "Like her dad who died last year in Afghanistan. I think she wants to know what it is like over there. She wants to feel closer to her father. She saw that sign for 'lunch with a hero' and her ten-year-old mind thought I could give her answers. But I can't. Looking at her face, I felt like a goddamn fake."

The combination of his harsh words and the way his hands had balled into fists sent a clear message—stay back. But Sadie couldn't. This man was hurting on so many levels it made her head spin. Yes, this was only a fling. They were two people who wanted a few nights, maybe more, of sex—although life kept interfering with the getting-naked part—but that didn't mean she couldn't help him when he needed it most.

"Look at me," she demanded.

Logan turned to her.

"Every person who wears that uniform is a hero. But

you're not gods. You're still human and you make mistakes. At some point you need to forgive yourself."

"Sadie, you don't understand."

"What you went through? No, I don't. But I understand Charlotte. That little girl's father was her hero from the day she was born. Serving his country, rescuing his fellow soldiers and giving his life—that just made the rest of the world see what that little girl already knew.

"But that doesn't mean she understood him or the choices he made," she continued. "She might spend years trying to figure that out."

Sadie watched the people below. Once again, she'd revealed more than she'd intended, more than she'd shared with any of her boyfriends.

"Sadie." He reached out and brushed a few strands of hair away from her face, his touch light as a feather. "Come here."

He drew her in, wrapping his arms around her and holding her close. She nestled against his chest, allowing him to hold her while her mind drifted.

Her relationship with her father was complicated. Deep down, she worshipped her dad. He'd done so much, given so much love. But now that the tables were turned and she wanted to help him, he pushed her away. She wondered if she spent more time with him, would that ease the tension? But finding the time while working proved a challenge. It was as if she was searching for a balance she could never quite attain.

Involving Logan in their troubled relationship was not an option. Not right now. He had enough weighing on him.

She lifted her head, raising her hands to his chest, slowly putting some distance between them. "Feel ready for your ice cream date after that little pep talk?"

"Yeah." She watched his lips curve up into a smile. "I think I am."

"Do me a favor? Don't eat too much ice cream. I don't want you to slip into a sugar coma and forget our date."

She felt the tension in his body change, shifting from friendly to intent. His arms tightened around her as his hands slid to her lower back. The untouchable barrier had melted away completely. He was hers again. At least for now.

"I won't." Logan lowered his head, brushing his lips against her forehead. Just once. "We have some unfinished business from last night."

His lips on her skin sent a rush spiraling through her body, alerting all her senses. She wanted this man. No interruptions, no hesitations.

"Tomorrow," she said. "I'm planning to get you naked first."

"We don't have to wait until tomorrow." He looked her in the eyes as he spoke, as if judging her reaction. "I'll honor our date plans. You have my word."

"I believe you." She rose on her tiptoes, touching her mouth to his.

She kept her kiss soft and light. His hands moved down until he palmed her bottom, holding her close—silently asking for more.

He pulled back and looked down into her eyes. "Don't be afraid to kiss me, Sadie. You don't have to treat me with kid gloves. I'm not going to break."

No, he wasn't. She wound her hands through his hair and gave a sharp tug before drawing his mouth down to meet hers. This kiss was hard and demanding. Relentless.

Her body pulsed with excitement. She traced a path with her fingertips over his chest down to the waistband on his jeans.

"Who's out here?" A low, gruff male voice called from the roof's access point.

"Not again," she whispered, closing her eyes. One minute more and she'd have had her hand around him.

A beam of light swept the area and Logan quickly stepped back, his hands moving to adjust his pants. He scanned her as if checking to see if her clothes were in place before turning his attention to the man with the flashlight.

"Officer Ferguson," he said, stepping into the light.

"Logan Reed. Shit, son, I saw two heads up here and figured it was some of the high school kids getting into trouble. I haven't caught you up here in years. Decide to lob some water balloons at the crowd?"

"No, sir. We came up here for a bird's-eye view of the crowd."

Sadie turned, crossing her arms in front of her chest. She was so turned on that she felt indecent. In the dim light, she saw an older man with a large belly wearing a blue uniform.

The older man gave a loud bark of laughter. "A view of the crowd? Is that your story? Well, you call it whatever you want, I still need you to come back down."

"Yes, sir."

Logan took her hand and led her to the door. Before they reached Officer Ferguson, he leaned over and whispered in her ear.

"Tomorrow night, no interruptions."

11

LOGAN ARRIVED AT the guesthouse and found a note on the door instructing him to come in and grab a beer. He obeyed. Three steps inside he found Sadie running around in a white towel, cradling her cell between her neck and shoulder. Waving him toward the kitchen, she mouthed the words *I'm sorry*.

Logan nodded, but he wasn't eager to give up the view. The T-shirt she'd worn the other night had covered more of her legs. He'd been on edge, wanting to get her back to where they'd been the other night on the couch. Only this time they wouldn't be interrupted by a trip to the hospital or a police officer old enough to be his father. Tonight there was nothing standing in the way.

Unless he got her naked and then realized he wasn't ready.

"Listen, Anne-Marie, I need to go," she said to the person on the line. "But I promise I will have a decision for you tomorrow. I'm not going to let this deal fall apart if I can help it."

Moving so quickly he wondered if the towel would fall off, Sadie brushed past him and into the kitchen. She dumped her cell on the counter before turning to him. "I hope we're not going to be late for our reservation."

"Nope. No reservation."

"Good." Her hands went to the top of her towel, holding it in place. "How was your date?"

He blinked and looked up at her face.

"Charlotte? The raffle winner?" Her fingers toyed with top of the towel as if she'd realized what she was doing to him, standing there, damn near naked, with the promise of sex tonight burning between them. "Ice cream?"

Logan turned to the fridge. He wanted to take her out before they lost their clothes. Pulling out a beer, he used the opener on his keychain to pop the top. "It went well."

"You can tell me all about it over dinner." She paused in the archway separating the kitchen from the hall. "Right now I need to get in the shower. I was about to when someone from my publisher called. We started talking and now I'm running late. But since you're here you can tell me where we're going."

Logan held the beer bottle to his lips and smiled. "Surprise."

She raised an eyebrow. "What should I wear?"

"Whatever you want."

Sadie looked him over, noting his clean jeans, T-shirt and cowboy boots. She nodded and disappeared down the hall, her hips swaying beneath the towel.

Closing his eyes, he rested his hand on the butcher-block counter. It was going to take a miracle to get through the dinner date he'd planned. Sadie set him on fire. And sure, a big part of it was the way they got so close that his body burned with anticipation, only to be interrupted. He'd been replaying the first night, here on the couch, over and over in his mind. The way her shirt had ridden up her thighs, the feel of her skin beneath his hand, the sound of her voice as she'd issued commands— If he didn't start thinking about something else he was going to need a cold shower before they went out.

Logan opened his eyes and set his beer on the counter. Outside the window, the sound of a bull kicking metal made him jump. His hand knocked the bottle, spilling the remaining beer over the counter and onto a stack of papers.

"Ah, hell." He sprang into action, locating the paper towels and mopping up the mess. Glancing at the paper, he cursed again. He'd soaked part of her book. Wiping the pages with the towel, the words caught his attention.

Logan froze, the soggy towel in one hand and her pages in the other. He should ask before he read this. But he couldn't put the paper down. The words drew him in, refusing to let go.

His hands hold my thighs, pressing them apart. His mouth hovers an inch above my bare flesh, waiting for my command.

"I want to feel your mouth on me. Now."

He buries his face between my legs and I close my eyes. This man—the one who burst into my life and demanded a place—he answers to me now. The heady feeling, knowing I control him and not the other way around, coupled with the first brush of his tongue, pushes me close to the edge.

He is powerful, inside the bedroom and out. His associates in the business world admire and fear him. But at night, he comes home to me. He strips off his expensive suit and kneels before me—the girl who once let a man take and take until she barely recognized herself, until she no longer knew the sound of her own voice.

I am not the quiet girl willing to let the men in my life walk all over me. Not anymore. I found my voice. And I intend to use it, in the bedroom. Especially there. I will tell him everything he needs to know to drive me wild. I

will not let him leave until I am completely satisfied. I re-
fuse to settle—refuse to let any man dismiss my needs and
desires. Not tonight. Not ever again. If necessary, I will
tie him to the bed.

   His tongue glides back and forth over the sensitive nub,
a thrilling mix of gentle brushstrokes and pressure.

   "Your fingers," I say. "Use your fingers."

   He runs one hand down my inner thigh. His index fin-
ger circles my opening before sliding inside.

   "More," I demand. "I want to come. Now. Like this.
I'm so close."

Logan set the beer-stained paper back on the counter.
If he read any further, they would never make it to dinner.
After that one page, he was about as close to exploding as
the girl in the story.

Staring out the window, he tried to count back from
one hundred. But it didn't help. His dick ached, begging
for release.

He shook his head. And to think he'd been worried she
was a reporter. But this, the erotic scene so unlike any fiction he'd ever read, was just as threatening. Maybe more
so. It was as if she'd looked inside his mind and discovered his deepest desires, things he'd never told anyone.

"I'm ready. Almost," Sadie said, rushing into the
kitchen. "I need to grab my purse."

Logan turned away from the window and watched her
move around the room, her heels clicking against the wood
floors. Her boots ran up to her knees, then bare skin up
to her mid-thigh. She'd chosen the same skirt she'd worn
that first day in The Quilted Quail. He didn't look to see
if she wore the same top. He didn't care. He wanted to
push her skirt up and sink down to his knees before her
spread thighs.

"Logan?"

"I spilled beer on this. I tried to clean it up." He picked up the papers, turning his gaze to her face. "Is this what you write?"

Her eyes widened with surprise. But only for a second. If he hadn't been watching her closely, he might have missed it. She buried her shock with a resigned look. Her hands fell to her sides and she dropped her purse to the floor.

"Yes. I write erotic fiction," she said. "I'm sorry. I should have told you. Before now. If you want to leave, I understand."

"Leave?" Logan let out a laugh. Walking out the door, away from her, that was the last thing on his mind. He'd read those words and pictured himself kneeling between her legs waiting for orders.

"I only read a few paragraphs," he said, never taking his eyes off her. "But the idea of a woman taking control and telling me exactly what she wants, demanding satisfaction, I have to admit that turns me on. Big-time. So, no, I'm not leaving."

SADIE BLINKED. SHE felt as if she'd been transported to another universe. He'd read her work and understood the needs and wants that motivated her character. He'd only read a page or two, but still, he saw it as more than a series of wild sexual positions.

"You liked it?" she said.

He rubbed the back of his neck, looking somewhat abashed. "Yeah."

"I guess you didn't get to the part with the whips." She wanted him laughing, not embarrassed that he enjoyed her writing. The last thing she needed was another person in her life who was uncomfortable with her day job.

"Depending on who is giving the orders, I might get into

it. I've never experimented with kinky stuff. Never really thought about it much. But if it turns you on, then I'm in."

Whoa. That was a lot of trust for a "just sex" fling. "You're serious?"

He nodded and she could see it in his eyes. This man meant what he said. He wanted to drive her wild and he'd do whatever it took to get her there.

The temptation to make him prove he meant what he said—it was impossible to resist. She stepped forward, raised her hand to his chest and pressed him back. He complied, retreating until his back hit the fridge.

Running her hands over his shoulders, down his arms, she entwined her fingers with his, lifting his hands over his head. She held him there. Rising on her tiptoes, her mouth inches from his, she said, "Kiss me."

She moved her lips to his and let him take over. His body strained toward her, but he stopped short of overpowering her and forcing her to release his hands. Running his tongue along her bottom lip, he demanded entrance. She opened to him.

His kiss was fierce and demanding. She moaned against his mouth, but he didn't let up. It was as if she could taste the truth of his words in his kiss. He wasn't walking away. Not yet.

Sadie widened her stance and stepped closer, capturing his thigh between her legs. Allowing her skirt to ride up, she rocked against his leg. It was crazy, but he had her so turned on, she wondered if she could come like this.

She pulled her mouth away from his and tipped her head back. Her breasts pressed against his chest as she rode his thigh.

"Sadie," he said his voice low. "We need to stop."

Her hips stilled as she looked up at him. But she didn't step away or release his hands. "I think that's my call."

"It is." His gaze dropped to skirt, which currently decorated her waist, revealing her red lace panties. "But we can pick up right here. After. First, I'd like to take you out."

No. The word was on the tip of her tongue. But curiosity—and the low growling in her stomach—won. He'd planned a surprise for her. And despite the very obvious evidence that he wanted her, he'd asked to take her to dinner first.

Sadie released his hands and stepped away, readjusting her skirt. "If you insist."

Logan nodded. "I do."

12

SADIE SECURED HER seat belt and waited for Logan to start the truck. It felt as if every nerve ending in her body was on high alert, waiting for them to pick up where they'd left off in the kitchen. And her mind? It was still in shock.

Logan hadn't run for the hills. Her writing hadn't terminated another relationship. Not that they were dating. This thing between them was leading straight to the bedroom. And he still didn't know she was MJ Lane, bestselling erotica author, who planned to go on national television in a few weeks. If he found out, he'd probably make a beeline for the door. But he was here. For now.

Logan started the truck and drove down the dirt driveway, bypassing the main house. Sadie stole a glance at his crotch. She couldn't help it. Anticipation ran through her veins, touching every part of her. He had to be in the same boat. One look confirmed her suspicions. Uncomfortably turned on.

Tempted to scoot over to the middle seat, she settled for reaching over and resting her hand on his thigh. Logan tensed beneath her touch, but kept his focus on the road.

"Where are we going?" she asked, running her hand up and down his jean-clad leg.

"Into a ditch if you keep that up."

Sadie laughed, but kept her hand on him, enjoying the connection. "Seriously, where are you taking me?"

"I told you, it's a surprise." He stopped at the main road. One way led to town and the other to the hospital, but beyond that she wasn't sure. "Close your eyes."

"Yes, sir." She shut her eyes. But she could feel the car turning to the right. The road to town. She'd secretly hoped they could escape Mount Pleasant for a night. The Quilted Quail served good food, but it was the only decent place in town, and overflowing with locals.

"Almost there," he said. The truck slowed and then took another turn, followed quickly by another. Then it stopped. "You can open your eyes now."

Sadie scanned their surroundings. The parking lot behind the bookstore, currently empty. "I'm guessing the store is closed for the night."

Logan nodded. He'd come around to open her door and held out a hand. "It is."

"Then what are we doing here?"

He led her to the back door, the one they'd used to make their escape, withdrew a key from his pocket and opened it. "I talked the owner into lending me the store for the night."

She followed him through the maze of bookshelves. When they turned the corner, Sadie froze. Her eyes widened and her stomach did a little flip. A table set for two stood in the exact spot where they'd first met. In front of the romance/erotica section.

"You didn't have to go to all this trouble." She walked toward the table, which held a bottle of red wine, two plates covered with metal domes and a single rose in a vase. "This is a fling, remember? I don't need to be romanced."

"Sadie, look at me." He stepped in front of her, blocking her view of the fairy-tale setup. Placing one hand on either arm, he held her there, demanding her attention. "I'm not ready for commitment. With my job, I might never head down that road again. But that doesn't mean you aren't special."

Sadie looked away. The honesty in his eyes—it crushed her. Despite his grief and the turmoil surrounding the mission that had gone awry, Logan was giving her everything he had to offer. He was building something with her. It would never lead to happily-ever-after, but still, he didn't hold back.

What did she offer in return? Her gaze landed on a shelf filled with MJ Lane's breakout novel—*her* bestseller. Secrets. One big lie by omission.

"Sadie?"

She met his questioning gaze, noting the worry making creases around his eyes.

"If you don't like it, we can go someplace else."

She shook her head. "It's perfect." She should tell him the truth, but not tonight. He'd gone to so much trouble. "You haven't told me what we're having yet."

He released her arms and went over to the table. Lifting the metal domes, he revealed two plates of sushi.

"Laurel mentioned it was your favorite," he said, setting the domes to the side. "I went with vegetarian rolls. The only sushi place is two towns over. I wasn't sure how well fish would do on the trip."

"Vegetarian works for me." She eyed the array of avocado, tofu and sweet potato rolls. On her list of things she missed about New York, sushi was in the top five, maybe top three. "Let's eat."

Logan nodded, walking around to pull out her chair before claiming the one across from her. He filled their wineglasses, then reached for his chopsticks and dug in.

"What about you?" she asked, watching him inhale one piece after another. "Do you like sushi?"

He shrugged. "Sure. I'm not picky. After months spent eating MREs—those are pouches of ready-made meals—I like anything solid."

"Is that all you ate during your ride?" She hadn't asked many questions about his horseback trip through Afghanistan. She knew it was a touchy subject, but she was curious.

"We roasted a lamb one night. And the locals provided meals. Most of it was pretty good."

"If I ask another question, are you going to tell me it's classified?"

"Probably."

"Fair enough." She picked up another piece of sweet potato roll. "How was your ice cream date?"

"Not bad," he said. "You were right."

"I usually am."

He chuckled. "About her dad. She started telling me about how he made pancakes and let her wear her princess dress to school."

Sadie focused on her sushi, not wanting Logan to see her face and the emotion written all over it. She missed the man who'd let her wear her Halloween costume to school in April. Her father was alive and well in Maryland. And she wanted more than uncomfortable phone calls. But somewhere along the way her money and his pride has driven a wedge between them, one that wasn't likely to go away anytime soon.

"You nailed it," Logan continued. "That man was her hero long before he put on a uniform."

"Did she ask about the war?"

He nodded. "She asked a lot of questions about what it is like over there. I tried my best to answer. But to be honest, the conversation moved on to other things. One minute we were talking about what it is like to live on a base in Iraq and the next she was telling me about her Girl Scout camping trip."

"Just like any other kid."

Logan nodded. "When she approached me after the raffle, all I saw was her grief. But there is a lot more to her. By the time we left, she was bouncing up and down, telling me all about her best friend at school and asking if I would come in and meet her class."

"Setting up a second date. Smart girl. Are you going to do it?"

"I might. Depends on how long I'm around."

He was leaving. Soon. She couldn't forget that after their candlelight bookstore dinner, they would eventually return to their separate lives. That alone made this fling doable. "How does it work? Does someone call you one day and say, 'Get back here now'?"

"Something like that. Depends on how Hunter, my teammate, does with the writer in New York. Probably won't be long, though."

One writer stood between him and what he wanted. Lifting her wineglass to her lips, she caught him glancing over at the shelves. The store's romance/erotica section was limited, but they did a nice job highlighting what they had. Many of the titles were face-out. Including hers.

Sadie took a sip. She wasn't the writer standing in his way. Not yet. But in a few weeks, if they didn't end their fling, she could cost him everything.

She set her glass down and pushed the depressing thought away. Tonight was for him. His chance to move forward.

"First time eating dinner surrounded by images of half-naked men and women?" she asked.

"The naked guys? Yeah. But you'd be surprised how some of my teammates decorate."

"Men away from their wives and girlfriends? I can imagine." He'd probably downed more than one of those MRE things in a makeshift camp filled with centerfolds.

"It wasn't the covers that distracted me." Logan waved his chopsticks at the erotica shelves. "I can't stop wondering, is one of those yours?"

Every muscle in her body tensed. She should have known he'd ask. If she was in his shoes, she'd be wondering the same thing. Still, this wasn't the time or place to tell him. "Yes. But I write under a pen name so you'd have a hard time guessing which one."

"Is that a challenge?" He pushed back from the table and walked over to the bookcase. Standing with his hands on his hips, he looked so serious as he studied the covers. Finally he reached out and selected a book.

Not hers. Thank goodness.

He flipped it open and scanned the pages. Color rushed to his face. Watching a man who looked like a superhero blush was a major turn-on. She crossed her legs under the table, squeezing her thighs together. Earlier, she'd been close to coming and her body hadn't forgotten. But tonight was his turn. At least, the first time.

"Tell me this isn't yours," he said. "I'm not sure that's legal."

She didn't know what he was reading and she didn't care. The man standing in front of her turned her on more than the hottest erotica scene. The way he looked, the way he cared, not just for her, but also for Charlotte—he spurred her desire. She was close to tossing aside her chopsticks and demanding he take her right there on the table.

Sadie stood and walked up behind him. Pressing up against his back, she rose on her tiptoes, her lips brushing his ear. "I can't help notice, there is no one else around. No waiters. No other diners." She reached around and plucked the book from his hand. "I don't think we'll need this. My imagination is running wild with what-if scenarios."

Logan nodded. "Always a good idea to run through all the possibilities. I'm listening if you want to bounce some ideas off me."

"How about I give you a demonstration?" She stepped back, breaking the contact.

Logan turned to face her. The man looked tense, ready to pounce. But he held back, waiting for her command. Sadie searched his face for any signs of hesitation. None. His eyes were fixed on her with a laserlike focus. His desire felt so strong, so present, it was like another living, breathing thing in the store with them.

"I think it is time for you to shed some clothes," Sadie said.

"Sadie, I hate to stop you, but we're in a bookstore," he said.

"I doubt anyone is in the alley. And this section is hidden from the front window. It's just you and me," she said. "So how about we start with your shirt."

She folded her arms in front of her chest to keep from touching while Logan drew his T-shirt overhead. He tossed it aside, but she didn't see where it landed. Those muscles—most men could work out for the next ten years and never look this good, this solid. Sadie's mouth went dry and her hands ached to touch.

"Your turn," he said.

The site of his sculpted chest and oh-my-God eight-pack abs almost had her melting in a puddle at his feet. Almost.

"I think you forget who is giving the orders here. Lose the pants and the boots."

Logan arched an eyebrow. He bent down and pulled off

his boots. Then his hand touched the button on the top of his jeans. She watched his zipper slide down. A second later, his pants hit the floor. No boxers or briefs. Sadie licked her lips, unable to take her eyes off the long, hard length of him. She moved closer, watching as small drops of liquid spilled from the head of his cock.

"Sadie—" He wasn't begging, but he was close.

Standing so close she could reach out and touch him, she said, "Hands over your head. Hold on to the shelves."

"Yes, ma'am." His tone was playful, yet heavy with desire as he followed her orders. He was enjoying this. There was no question.

Still fully dressed, she sank to her knees in front of him. "Keep your hands where they are. Don't let go."

"I don't know if I can do that."

"Every good soldier follows orders." Not that she'd ever had one at her mercy before. The men she'd dated in New York didn't come close to Logan's raw power. Their muscles came from long hours in the gym, not battling terrorists. The things this man was capable of probably pushed the boundaries of her imagination. Yet, he was here. All hers.

Slowly, gently, she ran her tongue from the base of his cock up to the tip. She wrapped her lips around the head, enjoying the salty taste of him. Wrapping one hand around the base of his shaft, she drew him into her mouth.

"Christ, Sadie."

Still stroking him with her hand, she glanced up at his face. He was watching her; his body tense with need and something that looked a lot like awe.

Sadie froze, her hand holding him tight. This meant something to him. It wasn't just about pleasure. Being here with her, it was a way to move forward and prove to himself that he wasn't drowning. Not anymore.

She'd only known him a few days. They'd both agreed this was a fling. Just sex. Nothing more. But there was more emotion tied to every action, every touch than she'd experienced, especially when kneeling before a naked man.

Taking the look in his eyes as a challenge, she lowered her head and kissed the tip of his erection. "Relax, soldier. You'll enjoy this, I promise."

"Sadie—"

She ran her lips down to meet her fingers. Moving her hand with her mouth, she repeated the action.

"Ah, hell, that's good."

She had a feeling that wasn't what he'd planned to say. But whatever it was, it didn't matter. She lifted her gaze, her mouth still moving up and down his cock, and saw him watching her. The way he looked at her—she ached to feel him against her skin, to feel his hands on her as he thrust into her. But not yet.

They had all night for sex. Right now, she wanted to give him an orgasm that made him forget the pain he carried around day after day. For a few precious moments, she wanted to infuse his world with pleasure.

LOGAN WATCHED AS Sadie took him so deep he felt the back of her throat. His fingers dug into the bookcase, itching to reach down and hold her head while he thrust into her mouth.

But he refused to defy her instructions. He didn't need the extra ammunition. Being in the same room with Sadie sent his body into red alert. Still, listening to her issue commands took him up a notch.

He hit the back of her throat a second time. "I'm going to come."

Without a word, she cupped him with one hand while

the other continued to work his shaft. Ah, Christ. Her hands teased him, pushing him so damn close.

Logan had his orders. But by this point he was ready and willing to risk disciplinary action to touch her. He released the bookcase and lowered his arms. Weaving his fingers into her hair, he rocked gently, keeping pace with her, no longer caring who was in control.

Sadie didn't reprimand him. And she didn't let up. She didn't let him think, not about the past, his mistakes, his grief that had hung like an anchor around his neck for so many long months. Talk about being at her mercy. Right here, right now, the sexy redhead who had burst into his life like a blast of C-4 owned him. And it felt good.

He exploded, coming in a rush. He closed his eyes and let his head fall back. She took everything he had, keeping her lips wrapped around him, her hands stroking him until he was spent.

Logan dropped his arms to his sides and locked his knees, trying his best to stay on his feet. She pulled back and he could feel her body moving, but he didn't open his eyes. Not yet. He was too far gone.

"Feeling good?" The commanding tone she'd used earlier had disappeared, replaced by her everyday voice.

"*Good* doesn't cover it," he said, opening his eyes. She stood in front of him, the look on her face a combination of sweetness and pure sin. Her lips formed a gentle smile while her eyes shone with mystery. It was as if she was running through a mental playbook of all the things she wanted to do to him next.

"Give me ten and whatever you're thinking, it's a go."

She laughed, the sound washing over him like a caress. "Ten minutes? What do you suggest we do while we wait?"

He pulled her close. Her clothes rubbed up against his bare skin, her hips rocking against him. If she kept that up he might not need the full ten. "You could walk me through what you have in mind for the rest of the night. Tell me what I can do to drive you wild."

She rested her palms flat against his chest. "You want me to describe it to you?"

Logan nodded, running his hands down her back to her ass. He gave her a squeeze, trapping her against him.

"Next time, I want you inside me."

"I want that, too," he said, his voice hoarse.

"But that is all I'm going to tell you now." Her lips touched his collarbone. "You have my word, no whips. But I need to punish you." She nipped his chest and he tightened his hold on her. "For disobeying my orders."

"You might tie me up?"

"Maybe." Her tongue ran over his nipple.

His entire body responded. Ten minutes was starting to look more like five. The way Sadie commanded his body blew him away.

"That girl in the story," he said, his mind still flooded with pleasure. "Is that you?"

Her mouth froze and she pulled back. Christ, he'd stuck his foot in his mouth.

"No. I've never been afraid to ask for what I want, or go after it, for that matter. But Isabelle—that's the character—she hit a nerve with women." Her brow furrowed as she stared at the books behind him.

"I think," she said, "there are too many women out there who haven't found their voice. I believe all women should go after what they want. Not just in the bedroom, but in every aspect of their lives."

"Look at me, Sadie."

She obeyed.

"I like that about you." He ran his hands up her back around to her front. Cupping her breasts through her shirt, he ran his thumbs over her nipples. "Tell me, Sadie, what do you want?"

A slow smile formed on her lips and the uncomfortable tension he'd felt a moment earlier subsided.

"What I have in mind involves a bed," she said. "Think you can manage the drive back to the farm?"

No. After his first blowjob in years, he could barely walk. But the challenge in her eyes had him nodding yes.

"Good. Get dressed, soldier. Unless you want to drive through town naked. I won't object."

She slipped from his grasp and he instantly missed the contact. He watched her survey the remains of their dinner, her hands on her hips.

"Do we need to clean up first?"

"No." He pulled on his jeans, carefully zipping his fly over his semihard dick. For the first time in more months than he wanted to count, he was ready for sex. He wasn't stopping to do the dishes. "I'll come back in the morning. And the store is closed tomorrow. Owner's day off."

He pulled on his shirt and boots, and then reached for her hand. Glancing at her, he knew. He wasn't geared up for just sex. He was ready for Sadie. Her laughter, her beauty and her take-no-prisoners attitude had a hold on him.

But he'd deal with the ramifications later. Right now, he needed her.

"Let's go."

13

LOGAN TURNED OFF the ignition and opened the truck door, his mind mission-ready.

The last time he'd felt this singular focus he'd been in a war zone. Right now, he had one goal—get Sadie into her bedroom and naked. Beneath him, on top of him, it didn't matter.

"Logan."

He had one foot out the door. But when she touched his arm, he froze and turned to face her.

"I know we rushed out of the store," she said. "But before we go inside, I want you to know that tonight was special. Thank you."

Her words warmed him inside and out, but did nothing to diminish his need to get her into the bedroom. Pulling free of her grasp, he climbed out of the truck and went around to open her door. Offering his hand, he said, "You're welcome."

Sadie smiled. Placing her hand in his, she slid to the ground. "Follow me, soldier."

Inside the guesthouse, he let her lead the way, unable to take his eyes off her short skirt. The fabric brushed the back of her thighs, teasing and taunting him. He wanted to touch her, taste her and drive her wild. They reached the bedroom and Logan closed the door behind them, locking out the rest of the world.

"I'm going to give you a choice." Sadie stood in the center of her bedroom, her hands on the zipper of her skirt. "The bed or the chair."

Sadie might be calling the shots, but he knew what he wanted—to feel her come against his mouth. After that, her body wrapped around his while she screamed his name sounded like a damn good idea. He could make that happen in the oversize armchair, but if she was giving him a choice, the four-poster queen-size bed sounded better.

"The bed."

She nodded. She drew her zipper down, letting her skirt hit the floor. Standing out of arm's reach in her shirt and red lace underwear, she bent down to unzip her boots, then tossed them aside. "Sit down."

Logan perched on the edge of the mattress, arms at his sides, fingers pressing into the comforter. "I'm not going to lie, Sadie. I'm dying to touch you."

She closed the space between them. "Where?"

His gaze dropped to her chest. He reached for the bottom of her shirt. His fingers ran up her stomach, lifting the fabric and exposing her torso. Grazing the underside of her breast, he paused.

"Here." Tracing a line across her body, he brushed the other side. "And here."

She stepped back, breaking the contact.

"Sadie." The temptation to pull her close, strip off her clothes and run his hands over every inch of her was at war with his desire to let her ask for what she wanted.

Slowly, she drew her shirt over her head, teasing him with every inch of bare flesh. Her red lace bra followed.

She hooked her thumbs in her panties, drawing them down her long legs.

Beautiful, sexy—these words only scratched the surface. She looked so perfect he ached to touch every inch of her. But it wasn't her breasts or the neatly groomed red curls between her legs, covering the part of her he was damn near dying to taste, that undid him. Sadie's confidence blew him away. She didn't hesitate. She was here because she wanted him. And knowing that she planned to tell him how she wanted him, in detail, pushed him close to the edge.

Abandoning her underwear to the floor, she moved between his splayed thighs. Sadie took his hand in hers and lifted it to her breast. Guiding his movements, she brushed his palm over her taut nipple before wrapping his fingers around her breast. She lifted his other hand up to her bare flesh and did the same.

"Touch me," she said, releasing his hands.

He squeezed, testing the full weight. Sadie moaned. Logan ran his hand down her torso around to her low back. Pulling her close against him, he pressed his lips to the space between her breasts.

"Tell me what you like." He needed to hear her voice, to know he was giving her what she needed.

"Run your tongue over me."

With one palm on her back and the other on her chest, he obeyed, licking a circle around the perimeter of her areola, staying far from the nipple. He knew she wanted more. He could feel it in the way she shifted, trying to guide his mouth to the more sensitive flesh, but he needed to hear the words.

Sadie let out a frustrated sound. A second later, he felt her hands in his hair, directing his lips to the center of her breast. "There."

Logan obeyed, drawing her in, sucking and nipping at the sensitive flesh. Sadie arched in his arms. He drew back, releasing her. "This is what you want?"

"We're getting there." Her hands ran down the back of his neck over his shoulders. Moving around the front, she began drawing his T-shirt up, bunching the fabric in her hands. She pushed him back and drew it over his head.

Her fingers on the top of his jeans, Sadie stepped away, pulling him with her. "Stand up."

He shifted off the bed and she undid his pants, pushing them down his thighs. Without waiting for her instructions, he kicked his pants aside. "Now what?"

She tapped her lips. "Stay here. I'll be right back."

"With your big bag of sex toys?" he called after her.

She paused in the door, looking back at him with those mysterious green eyes, her long hair trailing down her naked back. "Sorry to disappoint you, but I don't have a sex toy collection. I don't even own a vibrator."

"Sadie, I can't promise much. But I can promise you are not going to need a vibrator tonight."

"I'm going to make sure you are a man of your word, soldier. I might not have a bag of toys, but I can be very creative."

Logan watched her disappear around the corner. Christ, he wanted this—wanted her. But sitting naked on her bed, alone, doubt crept up on him. Was he ready? Whatever she had planned would probably blow him away. He didn't need toys. He just wanted her.

"Don't screw this up," he muttered.

Sadie returned with condoms in one hand. In the other, she held a spool of pink ribbon. Desire and curiosity pushed aside his misgivings.

"Planning to wrap me up?"

"Yes." She set the condoms on the bedside table and

began unraveling the ribbon. She wore a serious expression, but there was a twinkle in her eyes. Excitement. And it was contagious. He'd never gone to bed with a woman feeling so eager, not just for the sex—though he might go crazy if he didn't get inside her soon—but to see what she would do next.

"Lie down," she said. "On your back, hands over your head."

She waited for him to assume the position before climbing up onto the bed. Kneeling beside his chest, she took hold of his right hand and drew it over to the bedpost.

Logan craned his neck, trying to follow her movements. But Sadie straddled his arm, blocking his view. He could feel her hot and wet against his forearm. He wanted to pull his hand out of her grasp and slide it down, dipping his fingers inside.

"No," Sadie said as if she could read his mind. He felt the ribbon wrap around his wrist, binding him to the bedpost. When she'd finished, she gave his arm a light tug to test her work. Seemingly satisfied, she repeated the process on the other side. Leaving him tied up, she slipped off and walked around to the foot of the bed, surveying her work.

"Does this turn you on?" he asked, his voice low.

She drew her lower lip into her mouth and nodded. Without a word, she joined him on the bed, moving up his body, driving every inch of him crazy, until she placed one knee on either side of his hips.

Logan closed his eyes. He'd never been so hot and ready. And he had a feeling it had little to do with the pink ribbon. It was Sadie. There was no question in his mind; he wanted this.

He heard the rip of a condom wrapper. A second later, he felt her hands on him, covering him. Logan opened his eyes and watched Sadie shift over him, then lower herself down onto his rock-hard, aching dick. His hips pressed up to meet her, letting her take her time and adjust to him.

"Wow, Logan. Just wow."

She began to move, rocking her hips, pressing against him. Her hands ran up and down his chest. Her breasts bounced, demanding his attention. But he couldn't touch, couldn't taste. It was torture. He thought about breaking the ribbon, but then he felt her muscles tighten.

Sadie moved faster, shifting her hands to his shoulders and then to the mattress on either side of his head. Her nipples grazed his chest as her back arched. She threw her head back, closing her eyes and calling to a higher power. Then it was just his name on her lips again and again, begging him for more.

Her movements stilled until only her hips ground into him. Hard. She moved her hands back to his chest, sitting upright. Her wild-eyed gaze danced over him. He knew the moment she turned her attention to his bound wrists. Her body tensed around him like a vise. She raised her hands to her breasts, teasing and pinching her nipples, drawing out her orgasm. Forgetting about his hands and his desires, he lost himself in her pleasure.

The look in her eyes—it was pure wonder and awe. He saw the frank acknowledgment that he'd given her everything she needed and more. Watching her take her pleasure, knowing he'd given her what she wanted even if it drove him insane, pushed him too close to the edge. He focused on holding back. He didn't want to come yet. He wasn't done. Not even close.

EARTH-SHATTERING BLISS, *blast of pleasure, falling over the edge*—the words rushed through her mind. She'd described dozens of orgasms in the pages of her books. But now, as the sensations rocked her body, none of the words fit. She'd ridden Logan to an orgasm that had left her speechless.

When the sensations started to recede, Sadie squeezed her eyes shut and collapsed onto Logan's chest. Tracing his muscles, she ran her fingers over his arms until she brushed the ridiculous pink ribbon securing him to her bed. Seeing all that raw power under her control had pushed her to impossible heights, and the descent had been sweeter than anything she'd ever experienced.

Her face nestled in the crook of his neck, Sadie felt the rise and fall of Logan's chest. This man wasn't relaxed and sated. Not even close. Every inch of his body was taut, tense and rigid, struggling to lie still beneath her. Was he waiting for her orders?

Snap.

The bed shifted beneath them, rocked by the force of his arm breaking the ribbon.

"Logan?"

Another snap, and this time, he used the force to roll her body beneath his, without breaking their connection. His hips pinned her to the mattress, while his forearms kept his torso suspended above hers.

"Again, Sadie. I need to see you come again."

He pushed into her, setting a rough and demanding rhythm. She met him thrust for thrust, arching up, letting her nipples brush against his chest. The friction, his cock driving into her over and over, unrelenting, drew her closer and closer.

"Logan." She held on to his shoulders. Her orgasm threatened to shatter her into pieces. Her body was still reeling from the last one. But this time, he hit someplace deep inside her that took her further than she'd ever imagined.

Slowly, when the pleasure released its all-consuming

hold on her, she relaxed her grip on his shoulders. Above her, Logan stopped. She wondered if he'd come, but one look at his intense, grim expression said no.

"Again," he demanded.

"No, I can't," she moaned, shaking her head side to side. Her body quaked inside and out with the aftershocks of her second orgasm.

He withdrew until she felt the head of his penis poised at her entrance. And then he drove back into her. "Again. One more time. For me, Sadie."

"Logan," she gasped as he teased her a second time, withdrawing until she felt empty and needy.

"Wrap your legs around me, Sadie."

No longer caring who gave the orders, she did as he asked, opening up to him, allowing him to go deeper. She held on to him, watching as he thrust faster and harder, shaking the bed each time he pushed inside her.

He was so close, so ready to explode, but he was waiting. He was holding back. For her. Knowing that, she fell headfirst into another mind-blowing orgasm.

This time he let go. One last powerful thrust into her quivering body and he went still, moaning her name as he came.

Sadie held him, unwilling to break their connection. When the tension left his muscles, she drew him down to her, not caring that his weight practically crushed her. She felt him bury his face in her hair, and enjoyed the feel of his breath, slow and steady now, against her ear.

Eventually, he started to stir. He murmured something about the condom and then pushed up. She watched as he disposed of it and returned to bed. Lying down next to her, he gathered her into his arms.

"I'm sorry I broke your ribbons," he said.

Her fingers danced over his sculpted abs. "Are you?"

"No. Watching you come blew my mind. I had to see it again." He kissed the top of her head. "You can punish me later."

Knowing her orgasms turned him on to the point he literally broke through his restraints sent little aftershocks through her from head to toe. This man—what he did to her, what he made her feel—she'd never been here before.

"I'll have to find something stronger than ribbon," she said softly.

He nodded, but didn't say a word. Lifting her head she looked up at him. Asleep. Just like that. Sadie smiled, feeling the gentle, even rise and fall of his chest. She never would have guessed that trying to fulfill a man's bedroom fantasies would reveal her own. She liked him bound to her bed, waiting to pleasure her. But when he'd turned all big, bad Alpha male on her, calling forth her orgasms like a god, that's when something inside her clicked. She'd always wanted it to run both ways, but she'd never thought it would be possible. Until now.

"I like you," she whispered, knowing he was too far gone to hear her. "So much more than I should."

14

Logan woke to a buzzing sound and the unfamiliar feeling of something warm moving against him. He opened his eyes. One arm held the moving body close against his. The other rested across his face. He blinked. Pink ribbon decorated his wrist as if he were a party favor.

The memory of last night came rushing back. Sadie, naked, stringing him up to the bed so she could ride him. He waited for the guilt, imagining it would drag him back into the endless, lonely sea of mourning like a vengeful monster.

And…nothing.

It was as if he'd finally reached dry land. The sea, it would always be there, but it had drifted into the distance. He'd moved on and it felt good. Logan savored the feel of Sadie's body against him.

He knew his feelings ran deeper. He felt more connected to another person than he had in a long time, and it wasn't just the sex. Her laughter, the way she listened to him, it all left him humming with excitement and life. Hell, it felt as if the entire bedroom was buzzing.

Sadie lifted her head and looked up at him, smiling. "I think your pants are vibrating."

"My cell." He kissed the top of her head. The room wasn't shaking with excitement for him; that was reality interrupting.

"I need to get that," he said.

Logan shifted out from underneath her, watching as she snuggled into the covers and closed her eyes. One glance out the window told him they'd slept late. The sun was high in the sky, which meant that was probably Aunt Lou calling to ask if he planned on starving the animals today.

Pulling his phone out of his pocket, he glanced at the screen. Hunter, his teammate. Shit, this couldn't be good.

He held the phone to his ear. "Reed here." Logan crossed to the bathroom, pulling the door closed behind him.

"Hey, Logan. It's Hunter."

"Good to hear from you," Logan said even though he had a feeling this wasn't a friendly let's-shoot-the-shit call. "How's the shoulder? I heard you were close to a hundred percent."

"Yeah, I'm good. Fully recovered. How are you?"

Logan paced the tight space between the toilet and shower. "Good. Better now. I'm itching to get back to work." The image of Sadie curled up in bed on the other side of the bathroom door filled his mind. Wild, commanding Sadie looked like a redheaded angel when she slept even though he had a hunch there wasn't an innocent bone in her body. He'd much rather be in bed than talking to Hunter. But if there was one person he couldn't ignore, it was the man who'd taken a bullet because of him.

"But the R & R, it's been good," Logan added. "Still hate the reasons I'm here, but all in all, not bad."

"Look, man, I've met someone."

Logan stopped. They were teammates, like family, but Logan suspected he was the last person Hunter would call to talk about his latest hook-up. He had the feeling most of his teammates equated widower with monk. And they'd been close to the truth. Since Jane died, he hadn't touched a woman. Not until Sadie.

"And she's it," Hunter continued. "But I need your help. I need you to drive down to New York for an interview."

"She's it?" Logan sat down on the toilet seat. When he'd seen Hunter's name on his phone, he'd guessed something had gone wrong with the mission. But he'd never expected to hear those words cross his teammate's lips. Hunter had always been the hit-and-run type. No attachments, no commitments.

"I love her," Hunter said.

Helluva time for the team's playboy to change his ways.

"I know it hurts to think about it, but you remember how much you loved Jane?"

Logan closed his eyes and pinched the bridge of his nose. He didn't want to think about his late wife. Or how much he'd loved her. He was finally moving on.

"Hey, man, you there?"

"Yeah. I remember."

"I love Maggie," his teammate said. "The professor. The one writing the book. I love her and I can't stand in the way of her work. Not anymore. So I need you to come tell your side of the story. I need you to make her understand you were all kinds of screwed up over the loss of your wife and you made a mistake."

"I'm under orders to lie low," Logan said, knowing it was an excuse. And a shitty one. He owed Hunter. He had to talk to this woman. But revisiting his grief? He didn't want to go there. Not now.

"I know," Hunter said. "I'll handle things with the colonel. But I'm asking you as a friend. Please."

"Send me the address. I'll head out soon as I can. The drive should take six hours tops."

"Thank you." Logan heard the relief in Hunter's voice. "We're flying back this afternoon from Fort Campbell. We'll meet you at the house."

Logan ended the call and stood up. One night of sex that had made his fantasies come alive and now this. He left the bathroom, mentally running through the list of things he needed to do, including asking Aunt Lou to feed the herd and swinging by the bookstore to clean up dinner.

"Logan?" Sadie shifted to a seated position, the sheet wrapped around her naked body.

He went over to the bed and sat on the edge while he pulled on his shoes. "I need to go do a favor for a friend. I'll be gone all day."

Her brow furrowed. "Is everything okay?"

"It will be." Standing, he leaned over and kissed her, a gentle brush of the lips as if it was routine. But it wasn't, not by a long shot. What he had with Sadie existed apart from his day-to-day. She was all light, laughter and, after last night, the best sex of his life.

He pulled the bedroom door shut behind him. What would it feel like to make that wild, hopeful energy part of his world? To wake up feeling connected to another person again and again? Like a miracle. As if he'd hit the shore, left his grief floating in the water while he walked through paradise.

Except his past was like a weight, holding him in the ocean, threatening to drag him under. The monster in the sea? It was real and it was gunning for him. Only it wasn't driven by his grief for Jane. His mistakes, the ones he wanted to put behind him, were catching up with him.

And after Hunter's call, what had happened on his last mission wasn't in the past. It was his present.

Logan walked down the front porch steps and headed for his truck. With each step, he felt as if he was breaking that connection he'd found with Sadie. But even if he could close the door on his grief and that screwed-up mission, the paradise he'd started fantasizing about—Sadie in his life and his bed—would only be possible when he was stateside.

He slammed the truck door. He could daydream all he wanted; this thing between them wouldn't lead anywhere. Once he got back to work, they would go their separate ways. He wasn't dragging another woman into a life of constant deployments. He knew that was a one-way ticket to unhappiness and pain.

SADIE WATCHED LOGAN climb into his truck. He moved with purpose as if 100 percent focused on getting out of here. He wasn't running from her. Logically, she knew the phone call had propelled him into motion. But doubt lingered.

Was binding him to the bedposts with pink ribbons too much? Probably. Either way she refused to spend the day at the window, watching and waiting. She got dressed, laced up her sneakers and walked to Laurel's house. Her sister was home from the hospital and Sadie was in Vermont to help.

When she reached Laurel's back door, Sadie let herself in and followed the crying into the living room. Her twin stood by the front window rocking back and forth, the baby in her arms, wailing.

"Need a hand?" Sadie asked.

"Thank God you're here." Laurel turned around. "I need sleep. Here."

Sadie took the swaddled newborn, cradling her like she might break into pieces if she wasn't gentle. Lacey, her tiny little niece, screamed louder.

"She doesn't cry if you walk in circles," Laurel said.

"But I'm too tired to keep walking. She's been fed. Wake me in an hour and I'll nurse her again."

Hours later, Sadie felt like she was endurance-training, not babysitting. But the baby was finally quiet. Lacey had even closed her eyes for a while, but woken up the minute Sadie stopped walking. Sadie had learned her lesson. No stopping except when it was time for Laurel to nurse the baby.

She walked around the couch, past her cell phone resting on the coffee table. No missed calls. Not a single text message all day. Outside, the sun was starting to sink behind the Green Mountains. It wouldn't be dark for hours, but still, the entire day had passed and he hadn't called.

"He said all day, but I don't know if that means he'll be back for dinner." Her niece's big gray eyes stared up at Sadie. "Or after dinner. For bedtime. I guess I assumed we'd be spending the next few nights together. A fling is longer than one night. But maybe that was enough for him. Maybe that was all he could handle. Still, he went to a lot of trouble—dinner in a closed bookstore—for something that was pretty much a given."

Sadie looped past the table again. No texts. No missed calls.

"Stop looking at your phone. You're going to give my daughter a complex." Laurel stood in the doorway, her arms crossed in front of her chest. Her hair was wet and she'd put on clean pajamas.

"You look better," Sadie said. "Refreshed."

"I wanted to stay in that shower forever, but I figured you needed a break. Go home. Write. Get some sleep. He'll either call or he won't."

"I think I might have blown it. Pushed him too far for his first time after losing his wife."

"You can't blow a fling." Laurel took the baby from

her arms. "It might end a little early, but it is going to end eventually. Right?"

Sadie nodded. "Yes."

They would go back to their separate lives. She'd return to her work in New York and he'd go back to Tennessee, then off to the Middle East or wherever they needed army rangers.

"Bring him to dinner tomorrow night," Laurel said. "I'll judge how he feels. We can invite Lou so it won't look like an interrogation. She'll come to meet the baby."

Sadie shook her head. "Your baby is only a few days old. You can't cook dinner."

"I wasn't planning to," she said, walking in a circle around the couch. "I can either defrost something or we can get takeout from The Quilted Quail. Burgers and apple pie sound really good. Oh, and French fries. I'd love some French fries."

Bringing Logan over here, knowing their fling might have turned into a one-night stand, sounded like a bad idea. But Sadie couldn't say no to her twin. "I'll invite them and arrange for takeout."

Sadie left Laurel's cottage and headed across the fields to her temporary home. In the pastures, the cows happily munched on their hay. She thought about walking up to the main house and looking for Logan's truck, but she stopped herself. If he wanted more, he'd call or text.

Inside her quiet guesthouse, she sat down at her computer to write. Time slipped by. She stopped to find an apple, a box of crackers and a jar of peanut butter, but otherwise, she typed. And then, finally, her cell phone rang.

"Hello?"

"I know it is late," Anne-Marie said without a greeting. "Almost dinnertime. But they're walking away from the deal. The movie studio. I just spoke with your agent and she is doing everything she can to salvage this opportunity, but I'm afraid it might be too late."

No. Sadie refused to let the man she desired and her movie deal slip through her fingers in one day. She couldn't control Logan's feelings and actions, but she could do something to put MJ Lane back in the spotlight.

"Give me the number for the paper," she demanded. "The one that took the picture."

Anne-Marie rattled it off. "This might not be enough," she added. "No one will be able to identify you."

"But it will make them wonder," Sadie said.

She ended the call and quickly dialed. Even if a publicity circus erupted, what was the worst thing that could happen? She doubted a reporter would be able to track her to rural Vermont. And even if she had to return to Manhattan early, she'd done her part in Vermont. She was here for her niece's birth. And Logan? She'd helped him put his wife's memory behind him and step forward, toward his future. That might be all he needed from her.

Five minutes later it was done. She'd confirmed that the woman in the picture was MJ Lane. The man she'd spoken with assured her they would look into her claim. He hadn't sounded too excited. It was almost as if she was telling him something he already knew or had guessed. Either way, she hoped they would run the story, and there was nothing more to do tonight—except write.

Hours later, while Sadie was lost in her character's world, headlights shone in through the window. Glancing outside, she saw Logan's truck. It was late, nearly three in the morning according the clock in the kitchen. But he'd come back. To her.

A little voice in the back of her head wondered if she'd called the reporter too soon. Seeking publicity when he was under orders to stay far away from the spotlight left her feeling uneasy.

But this would never touch him. Even if they connected MJ Lane with Sadie Bannerman based on her tip—it would take time. They didn't even have a shot of her face. By the time they did, whatever was between her and Logan would be over.

Sadie stood and opened the door. Wearing the same clothes he'd left in that morning, Logan ran a hand through his hair. She'd spent most of the night finding the right words. Looking at him, only one came to mind. *Drained.*

"I saw your lights on," he said.

"I've been working." She stepped back, holding the door open. "Come in."

He hesitated.

Sadie cocked her head to one side, studying him. She didn't know the details, not yet, but she had a hunch the favor hadn't involved moving his friend's couch. His body radiated tension and his face was a mask of emotional turmoil. It was as if someone had asked him to hand over a piece of himself.

"I'm not great company right now," he said.

"Not many people are at three in the morning. But you look like you could use a nightcap. I saw a bottle of bourbon in the cabinet while hunting for snacks. Not much left, but I'll share it with you."

Logan nodded, some of the tension easing from his shoulders. "I could use a drink." He stepped inside, stopping in front of her. "After."

His gaze dropped to her lips. Shifting closer, pressing her up against the open door, he lowered his mouth to hers. This time, he was the one demanding the kiss, not with words, but actions. There was a harsh edge to his movements as if he was done holding back, physically.

But when it came to his emotions? The way he pinned her tight against the door, she suspected the only thing he wanted to feel right now was this. And she was right there with him, ready and willing to play, knowing the endgame was pleasure.

Sadie placed a hand on his chest, pushing him back, away from the door. It slammed closed behind them as she wound her arms around his neck. Holding his body close to hers, she broke the kiss and looked up at him.

"Last night wasn't enough for you?"

"Not even close."

"You liked the pink ribbon?" She said, her words laced with the doubt she'd carried around all day. "It wasn't too much for you?"

"No."

The way he said that one word—emphatic, strong— erased her misgivings.

"I liked driving you wild." He ran his hands down her back, cupping her ass and drawing her close against him. "Tell me what you want tonight."

She wanted him relaxed, laughing and happy. And she wanted him out of his mind with desire. But she knew that wasn't the answer he needed to hear right now. In many ways, they were back to the beginning, fighting all the things holding him back and keeping him from moving forward—emotionally, at least. Watching him freeze, unable to kiss her, that was the last thing she wanted right now.

The memory of that almost-kiss against her fridge brought back another. The shower. Him at her mercy. Only tonight she had a very different idea about whose hands would be pressed up against the tile walls.

"I want to get you wet," she said.

Logan groaned. "Feeling you tight around me sounds like heaven."

"We'll get there, too." She took his hand and led him down the hall, abruptly turning into her bedroom. She didn't let go until they reached her bathroom. "But first, the shower."

Turning her back to him, she slid open the door and started the water. Still facing the shower, she slowly lifted her shirt up and over her head. She tossed it aside and undid her bra.

"Sadie."

She stayed where she was, stripping out of her clothes while steam filled the bathroom, clouding the mirror above the sink. Naked, she turned to him. "You're still dressed."

He started pulling at his clothes, never taking his eyes off her. She watched, admiring every inch of him—all hers. At least for one more night.

"Come with me, Mr. Ruggedly Handsome." Sadie opened the shower door and stepped inside. Warm water rushed over her. Laughing, he moved in behind her, making the small space feel tight and intimate.

With the showerhead at her back, she faced him, raising her hand to her mouth. "Did I say that out loud?"

He grinned. "Yeah, you did."

Logan, joking and relaxed, stood in her shower, waiting for her instructions. The excitement was like a shot of adrenaline. She suspected it had as much to do with knowing she'd relieved some of the tension from his day as it did with what was about to happen.

"I want you on your knees," she said. "Kissing me."

Logan lowered his large frame to the shower floor. Starting at her inner thigh, he ran one hand down her leg. His touch pierced through her, sharp and exciting.

"Place your foot on the edge of the tub," he said. "Please."

Sadie obeyed, leaning back against the tile wall. Warm water rushed over her, teasing her breasts. Her body hummed with anticipation as he drew her hips forward, away from the waterfall. She watched as one hand went to her core, spreading her open. She felt the other arm wrap around her body. His palm pressed against her bottom, holding her in place.

"I've been dying to taste you," he murmured.

His tongue licked her entrance and she was lost. Closing her eyes, she let him command her body. There was nothing tentative about his actions tonight. He held her tightly, his mouth rough and demanding against her.

Her fingers pressed into the tile, searching for something to hold. She'd asked for this, but she'd never thought, she'd never imagined…

"Logan!" her voice echoed against the shower walls as the orgasm washed over her. If this was what the man could do with his mouth, she would have to find something stronger than pink ribbon to bind him to her bed. She might never let him go.

He released his hold, drawing his mouth away. She opened her eyes, watching as he rose from the shower floor. The heat in his gaze—that alone sent an aftershock through her body.

He reached for her. Placing his hands on her hips, he turned her to face the wall behind him. "Bend over and place your hands against the tiles."

One hand ran up her back, guiding her into position.

"Don't move. I'm going to grab a condom."

She heard the shower door open and felt the rush of cool air. Seconds later he was back, condom on and ready for action.

"Good girl, you didn't move."

"I can be obedient." She smiled at him over her shoulder. "When it suits me."

He let out a low laugh, and then she felt him, hard and demanding at her entrance. He thrust against her, filling her as the water rushed down her back. Right now he was 100 percent in control, taking what he wanted, what he needed from her. And she was ready to give him everything she had.

The night before every action had linked back to his emotional needs. But tonight? She knew he'd locked his feelings away for later. But she felt hers rising to the surface. Maybe it was the orgasm or the way he'd taken charge, either way she knew deep down that walking away from this man would not be easy.

Her core tightened around him as Logan's body smacked against hers. The orgasm built inside her. She was so close, she just needed—

"Touch yourself," he said, his voice rough and raw. "I need you with me. And I'm ready to explode, Sadie."

Moving one hand to the center of the tile wall over her head, she dropped the other down, reaching between her legs.

"Logan. Wow," she gasped. Her back arched and she squeezed her eyes shut, lifting her head back, feeling the water spray her face. Warmth, pleasure, it was all there, washing over her body.

"Logan!" For the second night, her orgasm began and ended with that one word—his name.

15

"You're good in the water. Maybe you should ditch the army and join the navy."

Logan swallowed his bourbon, doing his damnedest not to laugh. After what was hands down the best shower of his life, he felt too good to send the fiery liquid shooting out of his nose. Safely out of the laughing-while-drinking zone, he said, "What the navy does in the water? A little different."

Sitting cross-legged on the bed she'd tied him to the night before, wearing bright pink underwear and her marines T-shirt, Sadie nodded and refilled her glass with another healthy serving of bourbon. He'd pulled on a pair of boxers and claimed the other side of the mattress as if this—drinking in bed after shower-sex—was the routine. But it wasn't for him, not by a long shot.

Logan glanced out the window. The middle of the night was slowly giving way to early morning. "We might want to think about calling it a night."

She nodded. "Do you feel like you can sleep now? When you arrived you seemed on edge."

"Yeah. I was."

"This favor," she said, turning the glass around in her

hands. "It was bigger than walking a friend's dog or helping him move."

He nodded and drained the rest of his bourbon, debating whether he should tell her. Holding back felt wrong after what she'd given him earlier. Pleasure, comfort and, most important, the feeling that he'd moved on. After spending the day revisiting the past, he'd needed to know he could push forward with his life.

"I met with the woman writing a book about our last mission," he said.

Her brow furrowed. "I thought your teammate was handling the reporter."

"He fell in love with her." He turned the empty glass around in his hands. Little Miss Maggie, as Hunter referred to her, was head over heels for him. Logan had seen it in her eyes when he'd sat down to talk to her. Part of him had relaxed once he knew that what Maggie felt for Hunter was real. A woman in love was a lot less likely to screw over his team with bad press. Still, talking to her, letting her print anything about his mistakes, was a risk.

"He's putting it all on the line—this mission, his career—to be with her."

"Wow."

"Yeah. So I drove to New York and answered her questions. I told her the truth about my last mission. I told her about how I was still grieving when we deployed," he said. "It had only been a few months since Jane's death. I thought I was prepared to lose her. She'd been sick for so long. The pain and sadness—it took me by surprise."

"And you're generally prepared for everything that comes your way," she said.

Except Sadie, he thought. He hadn't expected her. "I am," he said. "It's my job to be prepared to handle any situation."

"Like showing up in Afghanistan expecting vehicles and getting handed a horse."

"Like that." He offered a faint smile. "I explained what happened during that mission, how I saw Hunter emerge with the blonde woman, the aid worker, in his arms, and I froze. I should have been scanning the area, waiting to take out the bad guys. But I wasn't."

He looked up from his glass, meeting Sadie's patient gaze. "One look at the woman in Hunter's arms and I saw Jane. For a split second, the grief came rushing back. I was lying in the desert, staring through the scope of my sniper rifle, and I was drowning. While my head was somewhere else, Hunter got shot. Our supposedly heroic ride ended with one of our own nearly losing his life. And that's on me."

"I'm proud of you for telling her." Sadie scooted closer and rested her hand on his thigh. "But what does this mean for your job?"

He shook his head. "Honestly? I'm not sure. Hunter's girl, Maggie, her dad served, and I get the sense she meant it when she told me she wanted to write a positive account of our mission. And it sounds like what happened, my mistake and Hunter getting shot, will be more of a footnote than the focus of her book."

She gave his leg a light squeeze. "That's good news, right?"

"It is. But if one reporter is sniffing around the story, there are bound to be others." He rested his hand on top of hers, craving the connection. "If I keep my head down and stay out of the spotlight, I should be able to return to work and prevent my team from looking bad."

She nodded slowly. "You love what you do."

"Yes." He looked down at their joined hands resting on his leg. A few days ago, he'd been second-guessing and doubting if he was ready to move on. Now he knew. She'd helped him find his way. There was so much he would miss about her when they parted. He'd miss her creative approach to sex, but her teasing, fun-loving nature topped the list.

"Being a ranger—it's who I am. I love serving my country," he said. "But it takes so much. So damn much."

SADIE STARED AT his hand covering hers. She had been wildly intimate with this man in the shower, but now? The fact that he was opening up to her, talking about his day and how his job impacted his life meant he considered her a friend, someone he trusted.

She felt the same about him. In a few days, this fling had started to mean more to her than any of her past relationships. If they took it further—

No. Impossible. He'd been clear—his position as a ranger meant everything to him. If a reporter discovered her identity while they were still together, unwanted publicity would rain down on him. And tonight she'd started the ball rolling toward her big announcement.

She wasn't willing to sacrifice her future. She couldn't. Her father, her sister and now a newborn baby depended on her.

"I've found that the best things, the things we want the most, come at a cost. Sometimes a job isn't just a job." She withdrew her hand, wrapping both around her glass. "I don't risk my life when I go to work. Not like you do. In fact, most of the time, I work in my pajamas."

She turned the glass in her hands, searching for the words and debating how much she wanted to tell him. "But I understand what it means to make sacrifices in order to follow your passion. Talking to that writer today, not knowing what she would write, took guts."

"Hunter took a bullet for me. I didn't have a choice."

"I still think you're brave. To tell her everything. To risk so much," she said, feeling like a coward. She should tell him that being with her could cost him. All it would take was one reporter snapping a picture of them together once the news of her identity broke. Then the press would start asking questions. Who was the man with MJ Lane? What did he do?

Logan should decide whether he wanted to stay, once he learned the whole truth. But she knew what was holding her back. He'd leave. And as much as it had hurt to watch Kurt walk away, this would hurt more. It was silly. She'd only known Logan a short time, but she felt more at home with him than she'd ever felt with another man.

"Thing is, I didn't." He looked away, focusing on some distant point outside the window. "I didn't tell her everything. There are some things I haven't told anyone. Before my wife got sick…Jane wanted out. Of our marriage. She hated the constant deployments. She wanted kids and with me gone all the time…"

One look at his pained expression and Sadie knew. "You would have given it all up. For her."

"Maybe. Probably."

Wow. When it came to personal relationships, Logan deserved an A+. Sadie clung to her job and the constancy it provided, even knowing it drove a wedge between her and her father, not to mention her romantic relationships. But Logan? He'd loved his late wife enough to consider walking away from his passion—being a ranger.

Suddenly, it became crystal clear. He'd meant it when he'd said he couldn't commit emotionally. Physically, he was ready. But emotionally, he was still in love with his wife, the woman he would have risked everything for.

For him, this was just a fling—a friendly fling, but it ended there.

"But I'll never know for sure," he continued. "I didn't have to make the call. Jane got sick and it was no longer a question. We needed the insurance to cover her care. Eighteen months later, the cancer won. My job was all I had left. Being with my team—there's purpose in that. I know the war in Afghanistan is not popular, but I've seen firsthand what happens when you offer people freedom and hope. It comes at a cost, and only time will tell if it is worth it."

"It is," she said firmly. She was doing everything in her power to offer one little baby a bright future, but he'd tried to make that possible for thousands.

"I know. I believe in what we're doing. I want to be with my team. After Jane died, I needed to get back to work. Watching someone you love die from cancer..."

The expression on his face was so distant; it was as if he'd returned to the moment when he'd lost his wife.

"I'd never felt so helpless. Sitting by her hospital bed, unable to do anything. None of the treatments did enough. She was too far along when they discovered the cancer. It was in her ovaries. After living through that, I needed to take action. I thought I was ready to be back on active duty. I thought I was handling the grief. But I wasn't."

He ran his hand down over his face. "I'm sorry. Unloading on you like this falls outside the parameters of a fling."

"So does dinner in a closed bookstore," she said. "You had a bad day. You're allowed to talk about it."

Sadie set her glass on the nightstand. Reaching over, she plucked his empty one from his hand and placed it next to hers. In a short time, they'd become friends who listened, offered comfort and something more.

Placing one hand on either side of his face, she drew

his mouth to hers. She brushed her lips across his, softly, gently.

His arms wrapped around her, holding her close as he leaned back, until he hit the pillow. She lifted her head and took in the exhaustion written all over his face. Resting her head on his shoulder, she pressed her body close to his.

Respect, friendship and desire—she felt all of those things for him. She could love this man. But like always, it came down to a simple choice—her career or her personal life. Could she risk her future to follow her heart?

Sadie closed her eyes. If she did, who would support her father and her sister? What about baby Lacey? She had savings thanks to her first book, but there was no guarantee it would be enough.

And in the back of her mind, a little voice said, *No, you love your career.* And she did. She wasn't saving the world or teaching special-needs children, but she loved what she did. Part of her didn't want to walk away from her passion for anyone. She wanted to find a way to be true to herself and fall in love. She didn't want to choose.

Sadie felt Logan relax as he drifted off to sleep. Either way, she'd probably never have to make that call. There was no sense in risking her heart if his still belonged to someone else.

16

SADIE ARRIVED AT her sister's cottage the next night feeling like a summertime Santa Claus. She'd brought the food—burgers, fries and apple pie for all—and everything the saleswoman at the baby store two towns over recommended.

"Anything left at the store?" Logan asked, eyeing her bags as he helped her unload.

"She needs these things."

Logan peered into the bag holding the high-end video baby monitor. "I'm pretty sure Laurel can hear little Lacey cry from anywhere in the house."

"But now she can see her," Sadie said, picking up the bag with the baby wipe warmer. She'd been a little unsure of that item herself, especially seeing as it was summer, but she'd purchased all the items the saleswoman had written down. When Sadie returned to New York, she wanted Laurel to have everything she might need.

Logan set the bags inside the back door, took the monitor box out and examined it. "Infrared night vision. Laurel is going to be more equipped than I was on my last mission."

Her sister burst into the kitchen with a screaming Lacey

in her arms. Aunt Lou followed. From the other room, Sadie could hear the television and Greg cursing loudly.

"What is all of that?" Laurel asked, eyeing the mountain of bags.

Sadie shrugged. "I had a few errands to run and stopped by the baby store you told me about. The saleswoman was very nice. She said you needed all of this stuff. I figured since the baby came early, you might not have everything. And you can return what you don't need."

"Oh, my God, thank you! Sadie, you didn't have to buy all this stuff. Having you here—that's enough." Her twin looked close to tears.

"Here, let me take the baby while you unpack." Aunt Lou scooped the crying Lacey from Laurel's arms and began cooing at her. As if she'd decided Lou had the magic touch, Lacey quieted down.

"Wow," Sadie said. "Laurel is never going to let you leave."

Lou smiled. "Logan, why don't you grab a drink and join Greg in the other room for the end of the game?"

"When it's over, we'll eat," Laurel added, pulling a pack of onesies out of a shopping bag. "These are so cute! And we're almost out. You just saved me a trip to the Laundromat."

Logan grabbed a beer and escaped. Laurel followed, insisting she wanted to put the baby supplies away. That left Sadie alone with Aunt Lou and the now sleeping baby.

"I was disappointed you didn't win my nephew in the raffle," Aunt Lou said, bypassing pleasantries as if they'd known each other for decades.

"I did my best."

"Five hundred tickets." Aunt Lou looked her straight in the eye. "I heard."

Sadie went to the fridge and pulled out a beer. "It was for a good cause. Literacy."

"Frankly, I would have preferred anyone to Charlotte Matthews. My nephew has enough problems. He doesn't need to deal with hers."

"I don't know about that. I think she might have helped him, too," Sadie said, careful to keep her voice low, aware of Logan's presence in the other room. "Sometimes it is good to set the pain of losing someone aside and just have ice cream."

"Yes, it is." Aunt Lou's take-no-prisoners expression softened. "Logan is a good man. A selfless man, fighting for his country and then Jane. It's about time he found his own happiness. A way to put the past behind and get on with his life."

"I'm not his future," Sadie said quietly. She was not about to tell his aunt that she was Logan's way to move on with his sex life.

"I wouldn't be so sure about that."

"He still loves Jane." There, she'd said it. Announced the fear that had been eating at her to Logan's aunt and a sleeping baby.

"Of course he does. He'll always love her," Lou said. "But life keeps going. Past loves take up their proper position—in the past—and the heart moves on. He's a good man, Sadie. He deserves a second chance at love."

Sadie nodded, realizing that was true. Loving someone in the past didn't rule out falling for someone new. But she couldn't be that person. Too many obstacles stood in their way.

"I've only known him a few days," Sadie said. *And we've spent a large part of our time together naked.* "That's hardly enough to build a future on."

"He's a soldier. Logan only has these brief pockets of

time before he goes back to putting his life on the line and serving his country. A few days, a few weeks, sometimes a month or two if we're lucky. It's not much. But it's all he's got."

The reality sank in as their conversation came to an abrupt end. Lacey woke up, Laurel reappeared in the kitchen and the men came in looking for dinner.

Sadie sat through the meal, half listening to Aunt Lou debate the merits of reality TV with Laurel. It seemed Logan's aunt had a weakness for *The Real Housewives*. It didn't matter which city, Lou loved them all.

Mindlessly eating fries, Sadie thought about Aunt Lou's words. *A few days, a few weeks, sometimes a month or two if we're lucky. It's not much. But it's all he's got.* Logan's life happened in fast-forward. He did not have the luxury of letting a relationship grow and develop over time.

If Sadie wanted more, if she wanted to see him again, she had to tell him. Soon. Before he shipped out, she had to tell him everything. And hope he didn't walk away.

After dinner, Laurel shooed everyone to the front room, insisting she and Sadie could handle the dishes. Lou eagerly agreed to take the baby. Greg and Logan followed.

"I need to tell him," Sadie said, taking a clean dish and drying it with the rag. "He has a right to know that I'm weeks away from telling the world I'm MJ Lane."

"Why? You'll have gone your separate ways by then, right?"

"Maybe. Probably," Sadie said, her gaze focused on the dish towel.

"Sadie, look at me," Laurel said. "I'm right. This is something more than a fling, isn't it?"

"Not yet." Sadie reached for the next dish. "But…"

Laurel held on to the plate, forcing Sadie to look up at her. "There's a but?"

"But I might have feelings for him. I might want more." Sadie shook her head. "Still, there are too many ifs in the way. *If* he's over his late wife, *if* he is ready to start a new relationship, *if* he cares about me—"

"He does," Laurel said firmly. "He cares. I heard he shut down the bookstore to take you to dinner. He cares. And he can't help the fact that he's a widower."

"Yes, you're right, Laurel. But this isn't a fairy tale. What if a reporter finds me here and takes a picture of us together? They might question who he is. His face and his name—he's under orders to stay out of the public eye. I should at the very least tell him who I am and let him decide if he wants to take the risk."

Laurel raised an eyebrow. "Mount Pleasant's not exactly a hotbed of paparazzi. And, honey, you're not Angelina Jolie. I don't think they're hunting you."

"No, I'm not. But I called the paper yesterday while I was waiting and wondering if Logan would come back. Speaking as an unnamed source, I confirmed that the picture they took of me walking into my building was MJ Lane. I pretty much guaranteed there will be interest in solving the little mystery of who is MJ Lane. And keeping that from him feels wrong."

Laurel's brow furrowed. "I guess that means you're leaving soon."

"No, I'm still here for you and Lacey. It is just one picture. And they didn't run it today. They might not run it at all."

"Sadie, if the shot was taken in front of your building, they know where you live. How many redheads live there? You? Maybe one more? If they quiz your doorman, they'll find out who you are. And then you'll have to go back."

"Yes." Sadie said. "But that will take time. And I was always going back. You know that."

Laurel nodded. "Then spend the time you have with Logan. Explore your feelings for him. You're not supposed to commit every part of yourself up front. Not in any relationship. Tell him when you're ready. But don't walk away from happiness just because you have a long list of ifs. Wait and see."

Her twin had a point. Sadie was already struggling to hold on to her heart where Logan was concerned. And he hadn't offered his. But he'd opened up to her, let her in, told her things he hadn't told anyone. Shouldn't she do the same? Even if it might spell the end to their fling?

LOGAN FOLLOWED SADIE up the steps to the guesthouse. Something was bothering her. She wasn't laughing or smiling.

"Did Aunt Lou say something to you?" he asked.

Sadie led him into the living room and sat down on the couch. He claimed the spot beside her, silently wishing she'd taken him straight to the bedroom. They didn't have much time left. Now that he'd spoken with the journalist, effectively removing the threat even if Hunter had led them down a different path than the one the top brass wanted to take, he expected a call any day from his colonel.

"Yes, she did."

Logan mentally ran through all of the potentially embarrassing stories his aunt could have shared. She'd raised him, so that list was a long one. But not one of those stories would have stolen away Sadie's smile and her laughter.

"She thinks that your love for your late wife is in the past," she said.

They were back to this. That word—*widower*—once again reared its ugly head.

"It is," he said firmly. "I'll always love her, Sadie. But I've closed the door to that part of my life. You've helped me do that. So did talking to the reporter, but mostly, it's you."

She nodded. "Good. I'm glad to hear that. But you're leaving," she said. "Soon."

The way she said those words, he knew they'd reached the crux of what was troubling her.

"Yes," he said. "I'm always leaving. That's the cold, hard truth of my duty as a soldier."

Sadie nodded. She looked on the verge of saying something. Judging from the pained look on her face, he didn't want to hear those words. *Maybe it's best if we go our separate ways* or *I can't take it, knowing you're leaving. Always leaving.* He'd heard those words before and he couldn't stand to hear them from her. Not tonight.

"Whatever you're thinking, don't say it." He reached out and pulled her onto his lap, her back to his chest and her bottom nestled against him. His lips touched her ear. "Tell me what you want. Tonight. Don't think beyond that. Just tell me how to drive you wild."

"I liked your skills in the shower," she said slowly.

That was all he needed. The future would wait until tomorrow. Sadie was still his—for one more night.

Logan lifted her off his lap as he stood. Taking her hand, he led her into the hall, toward the bedroom. "I think it's time to get you wet."

17

LEAVES RUSTLED. A branch snapped. Footsteps. Those sounds could only mean one thing.

Enemy.

Logan opened his eyes, alert and ready. Only this wasn't Afghanistan. He was lying in his aunt's guesthouse beside Sadie. He could feel her long hair, still damp from their seemingly endless shower last night, pressed up against his chest. Her naked body fit perfectly with his.

"Cows," he muttered, rubbing the back of his eyes with his hand. He slid away from Sadie, careful not to wake her. He needed to round up the escaped animals before his aunt noticed they'd jumped the fence. Lou would try to catch them. And when she did, she'd probably catch a glimpse in the guesthouse window. He didn't want Aunt Lou to find him lying naked next to Sadie.

Click. Click. Click.

Logan moved to the window. He heard the rustling again, but this time he knew it wasn't livestock. He'd never met a cow that could hold a camera.

"Shit."

He went to the bathroom and retrieved his clothes. Whoever was out there had spotted him and retreated. If he was smart, he'd be long gone before Logan walked outside.

Logan rounded the side of the guesthouse, moving silently over the grass. Scanning the area, he spotted a guy dressed for duck hunting crouching in the bushes. A camera hung around his neck. Another bag, slung across his chest, held a selection of long lenses.

For the second morning, Logan felt as if he'd woken to a nightmare, one where his mistakes resurfaced again and again. Maggie, the woman his teammate had fallen for, might be willing to write a positive account of their mission, but the guy snooping around his aunt's farm? Ten-to-one odds he wanted dirt, not a feel-good story about a war half the country didn't support.

In the field, a cow mooed. The guy with the camera turned and spotted Logan. He was on his feet in seconds, running. Logan went after him. He'd kept up with training while home on leave, but this guy was fast. It was as if he made his living running away from windows, camera bag in tow. By the time they neared the fence on the property border, Logan was close.

"Logan?"

He heard her voice and glanced over his shoulder. Sadie, wearing a T-shirt and underwear, raced toward him.

"Go back inside," he said. "This doesn't concern you."

His target pivoted, lifted his camera and aimed. At Sadie. This left Logan with a choice. He could block the shot or tackle the man to the ground.

Logan shifted right, moving in front of Sadie. Protecting her, keeping her free and clear of his mess, that was more important than taking this guy down.

The intruder lowered the camera, turned and started running. Logan went after him. But then the guy slid like a ball player aiming for home plate, and escaped under the wire fence.

Logan thought about jumping over, but a second later, he heard a car starting, then wheels on gravel. He'd lost him.

Sadie stopped by his side, breathing hard.

"You need to go back inside," he said. Not that the guy would come back. Logan suspected he'd scared the intruder away. At least for a little while.

"No—"

"It was a reporter. He had a camera." Logan shook his head. "Christ, I knew it was only a matter of time before more started digging."

"Logan." She placed her hand on his arm. "He wasn't here for you."

He studied her face. Remorse. Regret. It was all there plain as day. She'd been hiding something from him. He'd been so damn wrapped up in his own secrets and what to tell her, he hadn't thought to ask about hers.

"Come inside," she said. "I'll tell you. Everything."

She turned to the house and Logan followed, his mind running through the what-ifs. Jealous boyfriend? Ex-husband? Criminal past? She led him into the living room. "Before we talk, I need pants. Wait here, okay?"

She returned minutes later wearing purple sweatpants and carrying two glasses of water. "Thought you might need a drink after your run."

He nodded, accepting the glass. She settled on the sofa across from him. Days earlier, they'd sat in these same places. He'd been dying to touch her, his only concern that she would want more from a relationship than he could give. Lust—it was powerful. Caught up in a web of physical desire, something he'd denied himself for so long, he'd put on blinders, ignoring any hints that Sadie wasn't 100 percent open and honest.

Only this wasn't just physical desire. He'd trusted her. He'd told her things he'd never shared with anyone. He'd let this become more than a fling, more than hot sex. He'd thought it had meant more to her, too. The way she'd looked at him last night, as if his leaving would crush her, had said plain as day this was more.

But he had a sinking feeling he was wrong.

"What is it, Sadie?" he asked. "What led a guy with a camera to your bedroom window?"

She took a long drink from her water glass, set it on the table and folded her hands in her lap.

"I'm MJ Lane."

Logan leaned forward in his chair, resting his forearms on his thighs. Her words didn't mean anything to him. "You have a secret identity?"

"I'm the author of the *Isabelle's Command* series. Or at least it will be a series once I publish the next book. You've heard of it? The internationally bestselling erotica book everyone is talking about?"

Logan shook his head. "Haven't heard of it."

In his world—at the base, in Afghanistan and even in Mount Pleasant—no one was talking about erotica, at least, not to him. The fact that she was successful explained a lot, like her ability to rent the guesthouse and spend a month helping her sister. He knew she'd grown up poor, so he'd figured she made good money writing. But it didn't explain the guy with the camera.

"My book has done well. Much, much better than anyone expected," she said. "I'm releasing the second installment in the series next month. To promote the book, I'm revealing my identity. On national TV."

Logan sat back in his chair.

"The press has been trying to figure out who is behind MJ Lane for months. Before I came here, I caught a reporter taking pictures of me outside my building," she continued. "It was only a matter of time before they learned the truth, and I wanted to capitalize on the reveal. Control it. That was one benefit of being here, in Vermont. I didn't think anyone would look for MJ Lane in Mount Pleasant."

Logan raised his glass and downed the water, wishing it were something stronger. "I think it's safe to assume you've been discovered."

"Yes. I'm sorry. I should have told you. I would have, but—"

"This was just a fling." Saying those words left a bitter taste in his mouth, like he'd been hoping for more. But he couldn't do more. He'd made that clear from the beginning. He had to leave. Go back to work. Deployments and relationships didn't work for him. He'd learned that from Jane.

But, stupidly, he'd always assumed he'd be the one hurting her when it was time to end this thing, not the other way around.

"There's more. The other day, while you were in New York, I called the paper that had the pictures and confirmed that the woman was MJ Lane," she said. "But I honestly didn't think they would connect the dots and find me here. You can't even see my face in the shot. I thought my secret was safe and under control."

Logan nodded and pushed to his feet.

"It was selfish not to tell you." She stood. "Especially after you shared so much. And I had no right to risk drawing you into the spotlight. You've been clear that is the last thing you want or need right now."

"No, you didn't." Logan shook his head. He couldn't help but wonder—if she'd told him, would he have walked away? "Why didn't you tell me?"

"I wanted one last chance to be with a man who didn't link my name with MJ Lane and expect some sort of magical performance in bed," she said quietly. "I know that sounds silly, but it's the truth."

He wanted to reach across the coffee table and touch her. But he couldn't. He had to leave. He had orders to stay out of the press and she'd delivered them to his doorstep. This fling had to end. Now. But—

"Sadie, you are magical. It has nothing to do with your career. The magic? That's just you." He studied her across the table. She looked close to tears. But she fought to hold them back. "And I get it. I know what it is like to want someone to see past the labels. You're the first person in a long time who has looked at me with something other than pity." He rubbed the back of his neck with one hand, shaking his head. "But I should go. I can't be a part of this."

Deep down he knew it wasn't just the press that was pushing him out the door. He'd never held back. Not with Sadie. And the fact that she had, even if he understood the reasons, stung.

She nodded. "I'll talk to my publicist and see what she can do to keep you out of this. I'll leave a note with Lou either way."

"Thanks," he said, and walked out of the room.

Without looking back, Logan left the guesthouse and headed for his truck. He needed to get away from here. Clear his head. Decide if he should call his commanding officer and explain. Probably best to wait. Sadie would send a note when she knew more.

He smacked the palm of his hand against the steering wheel. In the span of one morning, they'd been reduced to passing notes. But he didn't see another way. It was bad enough he'd talked to the writer in New York. Of course,

Hunter hadn't given him a choice. And his CO knew about that transgression. This one was on him.

When it came to Sadie, he had a choice. Until one of them left, he had to stay far away from her. One photographer already had pictures of them. It would be downright stupid to take the chance again. If the guy he'd caught this morning published those pictures, it wouldn't be long before someone uncovered his name. Once they had his name, they'd learn his rank and position in the army. Then they might start wondering what he was doing sitting on his hands in rural Vermont while most of his team was back at the base.

Who knows where the story would go from there. He didn't want to find out. If he lost his job as a ranger, when Sadie returned to her world he'd be left with nothing.

Except feelings for a woman he couldn't have.

With his hand on the ignition, he closed his eyes. He liked Sadie. She'd burst into his life and lit it up like a firecracker. Just because it had ended with him still wanting more didn't change the fact that she'd given him the chance to move forward. He wasn't supposed to feel for her and want to turn this into something real.

No, that made him a fool, and that was on him, not her. Telling her things he'd kept from everyone else, even though he knew all the kinky sex in the world wouldn't change the fact that this thing between them would lead to a dead end—foolish.

Logan turned the key. He had to get away from here before he walked back in that door and put everything on the line for a woman he'd only known a few days. He shifted his truck into Drive and steered down the driveway. Logic was on his side. But he couldn't shake the feeling that walking away wasn't the right thing to do.

"THE STORY IS about to break." Sadie held her cell to her ear with her shoulder, while her hands struggled with the coffeemaker. "There was a cameraman outside my window this morning."

"They found you in Vermont?" Anne-Marie said. "That was fast."

The coffeepot snapped into place and started brewing. "I know. But it's too soon."

"Close enough. I'll call the morning show and see if they can move up your appearance to get a jump on the story," Anne-Marie said. "When this breaks, it could be great for your movie deal. It will be like Christmas morning arrived early for you."

Sadie closed her eyes. She was so close to having everything she'd wanted for her career. But—

"I wasn't alone," she said.

"Who is he?"

Sadie reached for a mug, her mind racing through what to tell her publicist. Just enough to quell Anne-Marie's interest, but not too much to provide a story.

"Someone I met up here," Sadie said. "A soldier on leave."

"They'll run that picture," she said, her tone matter-of-fact.

"I know. I need you to stop them." Sadie poured a cup of coffee. "His picture can't appear in print or online."

She didn't have a clue how long the reporter had been camped outside her window or what he'd seen. It didn't matter. One shot of the woman believed to be MJ Lane in bed with a mystery man and reporters would start digging.

"I want this, Anne-Marie. The publicity, the morning shows, the movie deal—all of it. But dragging someone else into it when he didn't have a choice—that feels wrong."

"I'll see what I can do."

"Thank you."

"But it might be too late. You should think long and hard about how much you're willing to give up to keep him out of it," her publicist said.

"I will."

"Can you give me more information to help track them down?"

Sadie told her every detail she could recall about the man Logan had chased away.

"And the soldier?" her publicist asked.

"Let's keep him out of this. Just focus on finding those pictures, please."

Sadie set her phone down on the counter and carried her coffee over to her laptop. Her twin's husband was off work today and Sadie wanted to give them some space. And she needed to write. The pictures, the reporter—that was beyond her control. It did not change the deadline looming for the third book in her series.

Work. It was always waiting for her. The one thing in her life she didn't screw up. For the past few days, she'd lived in a dream world, balancing her writing with her commitments to Laurel, and her desire to spend time with Logan. But like after any good dream, she had to wake up sometime.

It was as if she was watching her life pass by on repeat. Work trounced personal life. Again. Always.

A small, mirthless laugh escaped. They had that in common, she and Logan. Job first, love life second. He'd been clear on his stance from the beginning. And she'd thought it made them a perfect fit.

It didn't. It just meant that what they had together wasn't worth the risk. Lust wasn't worth it.

But love might be.

Sadie looked out the window at the clear Vermont sky. Either way, it didn't matter. He'd been here before. Logan had faced this situation: career or the woman in his life. In the end, the choice had been made for him. Still, she had a feeling he would have walked away from his job for his wife. But then, he'd loved the woman he'd married. And Sadie didn't doubt that Jane had loved Logan. How could she not? Any sane woman would fall head over heels for him.

Sadie closed her eyes. Right now, she wished she were head-to-toe crazy.

18

HER PHONE VIBRATED on the coffee table. Sadie opened one eye and reached for it, trying hard not to hope it was Logan. It was probably Anne-Marie.

Sadie glanced at the name on the screen. Her sister. She answered with a quick hello.

"You need to get over here right now," Laurel said.

"Is everything okay?" Sadie blinked and looked at the clock. Five. She didn't know when she'd fallen asleep, but now it was nearly dinnertime. "I thought Greg was home today."

"Everything's fine. And Greg's here. He's sleeping," Laurel said. "I need you. Now."

"I'll be right there." Sadie ended the call and sat upright on the couch, scanning the living room for shoes. She pulled on her boots, grabbed her phone, shoved the keys in her pocket and ran for the door. Ten minutes later, she was in Laurel's kitchen.

"What is so urgent?"

Laurel frowned, her gaze fixed on Sadie's feet. "You're wearing your city boots."

"They were the first thing I could find," she said, which was true. Mostly. She felt like herself in these boots. City girl. Career woman. After what had happened with Logan that morning, she needed a reminder. "You said you needed me. Now."

Laurel nodded. "It's in the front room."

Sadie followed her twin through the archway into the main living area. An opened box overflowing with little girl clothes sat on the floor. "Are those—"

"Our clothes," Laurel said. "Dad sent them."

Sadie walked over and picked up a pair of pink dresses. "He saved all of this?"

"Only our favorites. The top is mostly baby and toddler stuff. There's not much of that, but below I found some of our favorite dress-up outfits." Laurel sank onto the couch and picked up the baby video monitor. "Remember the princess dresses we got at a yard sale when we were seven?"

Sadie nodded. "I wore mine to school for a month. Dad convinced the principal it would help me deal with my grief over losing Mom. He conveniently left out the part about Mom passing away when we were babies."

"I forgot about that. You wore a tiara every day and made up all those wild tales about your royal family across the ocean who lived in a pink castle."

Her father had allowed her to live in her fantasy world, doing whatever he needed to do to make the outside world comply. Sadie stared at the massive box. A second one sat beside it. "It must have cost a fortune to ship all this and store it for so long."

Laurel nodded. "Now we know what he's been doing with your money."

Sadie sat down next to her twin and took her hand. "I'll get him here. I promise."

"Thanks." Laurel rested her head on Sadie's shoulder. "I miss him. And I want him to meet Lacey."

The imaginary scale balancing her career on one side and her personal life on the other might be leaning toward career right now, but that didn't mean she should give up. Not when it came to her family. Her commitment to her job strained her relationships with her sister and father, but it wasn't an insurmountable barrier.

With Logan, it was.

"There's something I need to tell you," Sadie said. "Logan found a reporter outside my bedroom window."

"They put the pieces together—your picture, your address—and found you."

"You were right. It was easier than I thought," Sadie said. "I'm sorry. I know I promised you a month, but if they publish the pictures, I need to go home. And you don't want a bunch of crazy reporters hanging around your house. They'd wake up Lacey."

"No one who threatens to wake her is allowed within a mile of my house," Laurel said, keeping her head on Sadie's shoulder. "And you've done more than enough. I know you have your life in the city. Go whenever you need to leave. Just promise you'll come back. I owe you and I'm thinking about repaying you in home-cooked meals. Give you a break from all that takeout you eat in the city."

"I'll come back. I promise."

Laurel lifted her head. "How did Logan take the news? I assume this means you told him?"

"Everything." Sadie stared across the room. "He was very understanding. But then, he just walked away. I knew he would. But still, it hurt."

"You're falling for him," Laurel said, knowing what was written in Sadie's heart even though she was trying her best to bury the feelings.

"I am," she said. "Or I was. It's over now. He shared everything with me and I kept one big secret that could destroy his chances of returning to his team. I feel horrible. But at the same time, if I had to go back, I think I'd do it all again."

"Because you love him."

"Maybe," Sadie admitted.

"You should go after him. Tell him," Laurel said. "You always go after what you want."

"I want him to be happy," Sadie said. And that meant letting him go back to the world he loved.

"What about your happiness?" Laurel challenged.

"My life's not a fairy tale. It never was."

"That's not true. Once upon a time, we were princesses." Laurel rested her head back on Sadie's shoulder. "You know there's a pair of matching pink wands in there. The ones with the glitter stars on the ends. We're too big for the dresses, but we could still be princesses and pretend that all our wishes will come true. Like we did when we were kids. Just for a little while."

Sadie lowered her head down, resting it on her sister's. "You're on."

An hour later, Sadie stood in a field by the side of the road, the heels of her leather boots sinking into the grass as she waved a pink princess wand at a cow. She'd stuck to the dirt roads on the way home from Laurel's house. Less grass to contend with in her heels, and much less chance she'd run into Logan tending to the animals.

She glanced down at her city-girl boots. Yes, she was the woman who believed in going after what she wanted. But she'd stopped short when it came to conquering career and love. When it came to love, she was a coward.

"Look where it landed me," she muttered. By taking the long way around to avoid Logan, she'd run into a herd of cows walking down the road. Lou's cows. Glancing around, she'd seen an open gate. Still, knowing where they'd escaped from didn't make it easier to get them back.

Prancing on her tiptoes to avoid sinking again, Sadie danced behind one of the heifers, waving her wand. "Time to go home. The sun will start setting soon. You can't stay out here."

The cow swung her head to look at Sadie, but remained rooted to her spot beside the road. She'd thought cows were skittish. Most of the others had proven her right, racing into the pasture to escape the crazy woman waving a pink stick. But not this one.

"If I leave you out here, you'll wander back into the road." Sadie continued her cow-herding dance while she tried to reason with the large animal. "Someone might take the turn too fast and plow right into you."

The cow lowered her head to the ground. Out of breath, Sade stopped her ridiculous jumping. "I can't believe Logan left the gate open."

"I didn't."

She spun around. Logan walked toward her. One look and she didn't feel like a coward for avoiding him. She felt downright stupid. Solid and strong, Mr. Ruggedly Handsome looked like a superhero come to save the day.

And she was the idiot who'd let him go without a fight.

Behind him, she saw his truck parked on the side of the road a couple hundred yards back. He'd been there long enough to see her jumping up and down like a fool holding a pink toy made for a child.

Stupid and foolish. Great combination.

"Don't tell me they opened it themselves," she said. "They're big and stubborn, but I don't think they're too bright."

"They're not. But they don't respond to magic spells." Logan stopped by the open gate. "If they'd escaped on their own they'd have pushed through the fence or jumped it. Someone left this open."

He walked over and hunched down by the grass. "Whoever did this drove in. From the size of these treads, in a small car."

Sadie started connecting the dots. Dread boiled in her stomach. "Another reporter."

He nodded. "That's my guess. Someone from town would have come up to the house or swung by the barn. And no one around here would try to steal a heifer driving a compact."

Guilt hit her hard and fast like always. "I'm sorry. I should have left after the first one showed up. But my publicist said she would handle it."

"It's not your fault. You didn't trespass." Logan walked up to the cow and gave her tail a twist. The animal jumped forward and looped through the gate into the pasture. "Whoever these guys are, they're determined." Logan closed the gate, securing the lock. "Heading home?"

"Yes."

He nodded to his truck. "I'll drive you. If you promise not to use your magic."

She wasn't a princess. Not even close. But pushing him away when he offered—even knowing it was the right thing to do, for him—her heart felt as if it was on the verge of staging a revolt.

Sadie bit her lower lip. This was her chance to go after the man she wanted, even if she could only keep him for a few more nights. She wanted to say yes and take that chance. But if she did, it would only make things worse and delay the inevitable. They had to part ways.

"It's a princess wand," she said. "And I can walk. It's still light."

He reached out, took her free hand and started walking toward his truck, pulling her with him. "I know you might think I'm a pushover because I let you call the shots."

No. Every time he let her take charge, she'd been aware of the fact that he could overpower her at any moment. And those times when he'd gone all Alpha-male on her, demanding that she come again and again? She'd loved it.

"But not when it comes to your safety, princess. Anyone who trespasses to get a photograph is a threat." Releasing her, Logan stopped beside the passenger door to his truck. "I'm not leaving you alone on my aunt's farm with a crazy person on the loose."

She put her hand on the truck door, preventing him from opening it. "We're talking about a guy with a camera. I think I can handle him. I've lived in New York City for years. You don't need to do this. To take the chance someone will take another picture of us together."

"I can't walk away," he said.

"I'm not a mission, Logan. Leaving me to fend for myself against a reporter doesn't mean you've failed," she said. "You need to protect your job. I understand, believe me."

"I'm not leaving you. Walking away—it was wrong. I was still torn up over talking to that writer in New York." He placed his hand over hers. "I can't offer you much. I'm not ready to commit. But I care about you, and your safety."

Not going after the man she wanted seemed stupid, but pushing him away when he insisted on staying with her? After he said he cared? She couldn't do it. Even if it broke her heart when it ended, at least she'd know she hadn't walked away because she'd been afraid of what she'd feel.

She opened the truck door and climbed into the passenger seat. After Logan settled into the driver's side, turned on the truck and steered back onto the road, she said, "If you're not leaving me alone, does that mean you're staying the night?"

He pulled up in front of the guesthouse, but didn't turn off the engine. "Or I could take you to Laurel's place."

Don't be a coward.

"No, I'd rather stay here," she said. "Laurel's in for a long, sleepless night."

He turned off the truck and smiled for the first time since she'd found him chasing the reporter. "Who said anything about sleep?"

19

LOGAN MOVED THROUGH the guesthouse, drawing the curtains and turning the locks. While he was at it, he checked the closets and behind shower curtains, anywhere a photographer hell-bent on snapping a picture of Sadie could hide. Once he felt secure they were alone, Logan headed for the kitchen where he'd left Sadie cooking dinner, making one last stop to retrieve a box he'd spotted earlier.

He'd spent the better part of the day pissed off while he walked Aunt Lou's fence line. At first, he'd centered his feelings on Sadie. She'd kept secrets. But as he'd walked alongside the wire fence, looking for breaks, anywhere a cow could escape—or a reporter could slip in—he realized they'd both been searching for something. He'd been looking for a way to move on with his life and she'd wanted a chance to be herself.

"Smells good in here," he said, setting the box on the counter. "I thought you preferred takeout."

"I can heat up sauce and boil pasta." She looked up from the stove and raised one eyebrow. "Monopoly?"

"I found it on the top shelf in the linen closet. Seeing as we aren't planning to sleep tonight, I thought we could play."

She laughed and the sound worked its magic, ratcheting his tension down a notch.

"You're on," she said. "Set it up in the living room and we can play while we eat. But I'm going to warn you, I'm good."

An hour later, he believed her. Seated on opposite sides of the coffee table, their empty dinner dishes pushed off to the side, Logan sipped his beer and considered his next move. He'd gotten out of jail, but unless he rolled a ten and landed on Free Parking, he'd have to pay rent.

He heard a rustling outside. Across the table, Sadie glanced at the drawn curtains, her body instantly tense and alert. Logan rose and went to the window, pulling back the curtain.

"Wind," he said. "It's dark out now. I don't think anyone's out there."

She nodded. "It's strange. The feeling that someone is watching me."

Logan turned to the table and rolled the dice. Eleven. He'd landed on one of his properties. "You said you were planning to go on TV soon."

"I am. To coincide with the launch of the next book in the series."

"Why?" he said. "If you're a bestseller, why draw the attention?"

"Increased sales." Sadie rolled the dice and moved her shoe piece to the next railroad. "And I'm also hoping to sell the movie rights."

"Are you concerned? About the fame?"

Sadie laughed. "It will be a hot story for a day, maybe two. After that, the mystery will be gone and no one will care. I'm a writer, not a movie star."

He rolled again. Five. Sadie's property, and it housed a hotel. He counted out the bills and handed her the payment. "What about your family? Are they on board with the media circus? Even if it only lasts a day or two?"

"Laurel supports me. I know she appreciates the checks I send each month. And if the tables were turned, she'd do the same for me." Sadie took the bills and added them to her piles. "My dad? I think he'd prefer his monthly checks came from somewhere else. He gets some benefits for his years of service, but he got out early and healthy, so not much. And he spent everything he ever made on us until I started working."

"I'm sure he's proud of you."

"I think he would have preferred I stuck with waiting tables, even if it meant less money. To be honest, I thought I'd be working in restaurants for a long time. I never expected my book to take off. I just knew I wanted to write.

"And my dad sacrificed so much for us that I want to be the best at what I do. Not just for him, but for myself, too."

"Did you always want to be a writer?"

"No." Sadie rolled. Another ten and another visit to one of her railroads. "There was a time, back in high school, when I was convinced I wanted to join the marines. Like my dad. But I had all these stories to tell and I realized I couldn't do both. Maybe some people could make it work, but I tend to throw myself into something one hundred percent. In this case, writing."

"A good quality." He took the dice, but didn't roll. If he landed on her property one more time, the game would be over. He wasn't ready to stop playing yet. "You would have made a great marine."

"Maybe." She cocked her head. "What about you? Why did you join the army?"

"I didn't want to be a farmer my entire life. I like raising cows and working Aunt Lou's land. I'll probably move back here and take over for her one day, but I wanted to get out for a while." He looked down at the dice in his hand. "I also lost a few friends. On 9/11. We were just out of college and a couple of guys I knew went to work on Wall Street, to get away from Vermont for a while. I'd moved back home, married and was settling down. Only I wasn't settled. I wanted more.

"After I joined, I set my sights on becoming a ranger." He shrugged. "Then, I didn't want to leave. Still don't. I'm not ready to trade jumping out of helicopters and riding horses through war zones for herding cows full-time. I love my job, Sadie."

She nodded. Logan waited for her to press for more, ask about when Jane demanded that he choose between his marriage and his career. She was probably wondering if he'd been up for farm life then. The answer was no, he hadn't been ready. But he likely would have left anyway. He knew it didn't reflect well on him that he probably would have held it against her, and their marriage might have failed anyway.

"It's your turn." She nodded her head toward the dice in his hand.

Just like that she let the subject drop, accepting he'd tell her when he could.

"I have a bad feeling about this one." He rolled and, sure enough, landed on another one of her properties. "I can't pay the rent. I'm out of cash. So that's it. Game over."

Sadie smiled, her eyes sparkling like a cat that'd caught a mouse. "I'll take your shirt."

Logan raised an eyebrow. "Strip Monopoly?"

"I'm going to get you out of it sooner or later, might as well hand it over now."

He reached behind him and pulled his T-shirt over his head. Balling it up, he tossed it at her.

Sadie caught it and set it down by her side, not once

looking away. "The way you look without your shirt? I like that about you."

Logan laughed, the tension easing from his body. It was as if Sadie sensed his limits and respected them. She understood he didn't want to focus on pain, loss and the past. He wanted to laugh. And right now, get naked. With her.

"I could keep rolling the dice, sacrificing an article of clothing each time," he said. "Or I could hand over everything right now and crown you the winner."

Her eyes widened. "For a soldier you certainly wave the white flag quickly."

"I think it is worth sacrificing my freedom to be your prisoner."

She looked him over. "Okay, soldier, I'll take your socks."

Logan pushed to his feet. One by one, he removed his socks and tossed them at her. "Next?"

She tapped one finger to her pursed lips. Every time she did that, he remembered the bookstore—that first day when he'd run into her and she'd teased and joked with him. "Not much left," she said. "I think it is time to hand over your pants."

Logan unbuttoned his jeans, and then slowly drew the zipper down. He hooked his thumbs in the top of his boxers and pulled them down with his jeans. Stepping out of his pants, he kicked them over to her.

Sadie pushed them aside as she rose up on her knees and inched over to him. Outside, he heard another rustling, but this time, he didn't think about investigating, not with her mouth inches from his dick.

Grabbing hold of his hips, she leaned forward and ran her tongue over him. Logan closed his eyes. He'd been a fool to walk away from her, from this. Even if it couldn't last.

She drew back. "Hold that thought."

She was on her feet and heading for the hall when he opened his eyes. "Sadie, no one's out there."

She walked back through the archway and held out her hand. The pink ribbon. "Your turn to call the shots. Tonight, I'm your prisoner. After all, I'd hate for you to feel like a pushover."

He took the spool, turning it over in his hands. "You know, I never asked, what is your fantasy? Not what you write about, but what turns you on?"

Sadie blinked. "My fantasy?"

The way she said the words, he wondered if anyone had ever posed the question to her. Or had they simply assumed what she wrote and what she wanted were one and the same, even though the character in her book was nothing like her? Sadie stood her ground. She made demands. She wasn't searching for her voice; she'd found it.

Sadie took the ribbon back and tossed it on the couch. Pressing her clothed body against his naked one, she pushed up on her tiptoes and kissed him, gently. "You. I just want you. That's my fantasy. My fairy tale."

Taking his hand, she led him down the hall to her bedroom. Logan kicked the door closed behind them, reaching for Sadie, pulling her clothes off. He needed to feel her, touch her—make love to her.

"As you wish, princess," he said, guiding her to the bed. He lowered her down when the back of her knees hit the mattress. Without taking his eyes off her, he moved around to the nightstand, retrieved a condom and covered himself. She ran her hands over her breasts, teasing her nipples with her fingers, while she waited.

"You're killing me, Sadie. Watching you touch yourself…" He shook his head.

"I thought you liked knowing what turns me on?"

"I do." Returning to the edge of the bed, he captured

her wrists, one in each hand, and drew them away from her chest. "But I also want to be inside you when I come."

Slowly, he lowered himself down on top of her, suspending his weight on his arms. The feel of her skin brushing his, the way she pressed against him, begging and pleading with every movement for more—he couldn't walk away from this, from her. He knew he had to, but right now it felt impossible.

"Sadie," he said, brushing his lips over hers. "This is more than a fling."

She nodded, pushing her hips up into him. "I know."

"You surprise me, at every turn, always offering something unexpected." He closed his eyes, savoring the feel of her nipples brushing back and forth against his chest. Her smooth legs wrapped tight around him, holding him captive. If only he could stay here like this, with her. "I wish I could give you more. I want to make promises, but—"

"Our lives are moving full-speed ahead in different directions," she said.

"Even if they weren't…" He shook his head.

Committing to her meant dragging her into his world of deployments and waiting. She wouldn't know where he was or if he was even alive. He couldn't call her with updates. He wouldn't be able to tell her anything. She was strong, so strong, but he'd witnessed firsthand what the separation and waiting could do. What if he brought Sadie into his world and the waiting crushed her spirit? Her laughter?

"I'm not sure I could give you more," he said. "A real relationship."

Sadie lowered her legs, releasing her hold on him. She reached between them, taking him in her hand and positioning him at her entrance. She rocked her hips forward, opening to him, drawing him in. "This is real. Whatever this is, it's real and it's enough. For tonight."

Logan kissed her deeply. Her legs wound around his hips again, moving against him, making love to him, offering everything she had. Unable to hold back, he thrust, harder and faster, his movements pushing her body up the bed.

"I need you with me, Sadie," he said. "Tell me you're with me."

"I'm with you."

She was. He could feel her tightening around him. She was so close. One more thrust—

"Logan!"

His name on her lips—that did it for him. He came hard, pouring everything he had to give into her.

Afterward, lying in bed with Sadie curled against his side, he wondered how much he was willing to give up. His job? His heart? What would it take to make what they'd shared enough not just for tonight, but for the future? And was he ready to go there?

20

SADIE WOKE UP and reached for Logan, patting the pillow beside her. Nothing. She opened one eye and saw a yellow Post-it. Sitting up, she read the note. "Gone to feed the herd. Coffee is in the kitchen. Don't open the curtains or unlock the doors until I get back." Sadie smiled, slipping out of bed to find her robe. Last night he'd confirmed something she had been afraid to admit due to all the ifs in the way. They'd tumbled into relationship territory. She'd known for a while her feelings for him ran beyond hot and heavy vacation sex. Somewhere between dinner in the bookstore and finding the reporter, this had stopped being a fling. For her, it came perilously close to love. What would it take for him to see that this was a real relationship, she wondered, one worth pursuing?

Filling her mug, Sadie heard her phone vibrate. She walked into the living room, still dark with the curtains drawn, and found her cell.

"Hi, Dad," she said.

"If your offer is still on the table, I'd like to book a flight to Vermont," he said gruffly. "I'd like to meet my granddaughter."

"If you want, you can use my credit card to book the flight. Do you still have the number?"

There was a pause and Sadie feared she'd pushed too hard.

"I do," he said.

"Book a flight. Stay for as long as you want. There's a spare room in the guesthouse."

"I don't want to get in your way."

"You won't." She couldn't play strip Monopoly in the living room with Logan, but she'd manage. She wanted her father here. After last night, she was starting to feel as if she could do anything—pursue love, mend fences with her father and tell the world she was MJ Lane.

"If you're sure," her father said.

"I am, Daddy. And thank you for sending our wands."

"You were always my little princesses. You and Laurel." He laughed, and for the first time in what felt like forever, the tension between them drifted away. Not far, but a brief reprieve. "Good thing I saved them."

"Yes. It meant a lot to us," she said. "I can't wait to see you, Daddy. I love you."

"I love you, too, princess."

Sadie ended the call and opened her laptop. Sipping her coffee, she logged into her bank account and transferred money to her father's account. She didn't want him worrying about missed income while he was visiting.

Her family would be together again. Maybe she could convince her father to move here. Instead of finding another job, he could help Laurel with the baby. That would allow her twin to start looking for another position. She knew being unemployed bothered Laurel, but the cost of child care would take most of what her sister would make. If her father moved here, and Sadie covered his living expenses, it would be a win-win. Maybe Lou would consider renting the guesthouse long-term. With two bedrooms, Sadie could make regular visits to see her family.

And Logan.

Except Logan wouldn't be here. He'd be deployed with his team or in Tennessee, near his base.

Sadie stared out the window at the seemingly endless green fields. What if she met him halfway? Keeping what they had, moving it to the next level—it was about compromise. So, what was she willing to give up?

New York? Probably. She could write anywhere. Her career? No. An imaginary roadblock appeared on the fairytale road to happy-ever-after in her mind. And then there was the small issue of those pictures. She hadn't heard from Anne-Marie yet. They might not be able to stop the story.

Still, after last night she had to wonder if there was a way around, a detour. She and Logan could discuss it together, she decided, when he returned from feeding the animals. They could brainstorm options. If he was ready to let her into his heart, if he was open to a second chance at love, to borrow his aunt's words, they could find a way to make this work. And after the way he'd made love to her last night, she suspected he might be close.

Sadie opened her email and scanned her inbox. A Google Alert notification for MJ Lane caught her attention. She clicked on the message and read the one-line description—Bestselling erotica author discovered in Vermont. Trying out new scenes? You be the judge.

No, no, no!

She moved her mouse over the link, took a deep breath and clicked. A tabloid's homepage filled her screen. Picture after picture of her with Logan. That man with the camera—he hadn't just been hiding outside her window, he'd been in town for days, long before she'd called in the tip to the paper. Someone had connected the dots between the redhead hiding her face and Sadie Bannerman, and found her here, in Vermont. He'd followed her. Everywhere. And not just her, Logan, too.

The top one—it was the most damning, and by far the most invasive breach of privacy. Sadie bit her lip. She'd told Logan she'd welcome the fame. She'd done everything she could to go after it and secure her movie deal. But this? She'd never imagined something like this would happen.

Staring at the image, she felt as if something had been stolen from her. The photographer must have hidden among the garbage bins in the side alley and climbed up on a crate or something to get the shot. That moment, when she'd stripped Logan down and demanded he hold on to the shelves while she knelt in front of him, that belonged to her, to them. But here it was, posted on the internet for the world to see. The caption below the shot read *MJ Lane Blows Her Mystery Man Away.*

Tears welled in her eyes. Not for herself. Let the world see her giving a man a blow job. She didn't care. But Logan? This could ruin him. This picture could strip away his career, his future.

Sadie forced herself to look at all of the images. The next one showed Logan at her doorstep in the middle of the night. He looked broken and desperate. In the next frame, he had her pinned up against the door. The final shot before the two-paragraph "story" featured Logan at the ice cream parlor sitting across from a little girl. Charlotte. They'd been careful not to show her face. But the caption? *MJ Lane's Lover a Father?*

Sadie's stomach churned and she feared she was going to be sick. That shot—it would kill him. He'd been clear the night of the festival that he felt like an impostor compared to the father Charlotte had loved and lost.

This wasn't just a roadblock to a relationship. These pictures were a dead end at the edge of a cliff. There was no way forward and no way back. Not once he saw this.

Sadie gripped her coffee mug, her hands shaking. She'd wanted publicity. But not like this. Not at the expense of an innocent little girl. Not at the expense of the man Sadie was falling for.

Next to her computer, her phone vibrated. Sadie glanced at the screen, afraid of what she'd see. But it was a text from Laurel.

Can u pick up diapers? Hate to ask, but we are almost out. I'll pay u back. Greg gets paid this week.

She stared at the words for a second before responding with a quick yes. Feeling numb, needing to take action on something, she went online and ordered three cases of diapers—one newborn and two in the next size up. She ordered baby food, bottles and sippy cups, toys and books—anything and everything her little niece might need. She entered her credit card information and hit Submit on the order without looking at the total bill. She could afford it. Her success provided for her family. And that's what she wanted, right? Even if it cost her a chance with the man she wanted in her life, loving her and accepting her love in return.

The phone buzzed again and this time it wasn't a text. It was Anne-Marie.

"I thought you were going to keep those pictures out of the media," Sadie snapped, knowing she deserved her share of the blame.

"I did my best. The photographer was a freelancer and sold everything to the highest bidder. In this case, a tabloid. I have no pull there.

"Look on the bright side, no one reported MJ Lane is Sadie Bannerman," her publicist continued. "We still have a story. For at least the next twenty-four hours. I've booked you on a major national morning show. The prime-time slot, tomorrow morning. Sadie, this is what you wanted. Maybe not those pictures per se—"

"There is a child in one of these shots!" Sadie exclaimed. "A little girl who lost her father to an IED blast."

"I know, but the story is out there. Do the morning show. This is your chance to explain. Tell them you're in love with this mystery man. Explain about the little girl's father and why she is having ice cream with your lover. Have your say."

Sadie pushed back from the table and started pacing. She felt caged, trapped by the media she'd actively pursued. Her publicist's words made sense. She had to set the story straight. This was no longer about selling books and elevating the career that supported her family. Logan's future was at stake. An innocent child had been dragged into the mess. If she did this interview, maybe, just maybe, she could save Logan's job and keep the press from speculating further about Charlotte.

But first, she had to discuss it with him. She owed him that much.

"I'll think about it."

"I need an answer, Sadie. In two hours. I can't hold them off longer than that. They'll require time to prepare the segment."

"If I agree to do this, will the interview be about my secret identity and my books, or about those pictures?"

"One way or another, if you do the show you're going to have to talk about the man in those pictures. What you say is up to you. But the more you share, the bigger the boost for your career."

"You'll have my answer in two hours."

LOGAN TOSSED A bale of hay over the fence into Titan's pen. He picked up the wheelbarrow and steered it toward the heifers' pasture. Last delivery and then he could return to Sadie. If he was lucky, she'd still be in bed, naked, her long red hair covering the pillows. He was ready and willing to report for duty, hand over the pink ribbon and follow her orders.

He glanced at the sun rising high in the sky. The chances of finding her in bed were slim. If she was awake, they should talk first. They needed to have a conversation about where this thing between them was headed. And it needed to happen when he wasn't inside her, making love to her— or bound to the bedpost.

He'd been thinking long and hard all morning while feeding the animals. It wasn't fair for him to unilaterally decide Sadie couldn't handle the deployments. He owed it to her to explain what was holding him back, what his misgivings were and hear her thoughts. They'd only known each other a matter of days, but she already felt like family, like home. He couldn't walk away from her without at least giving a long-term relationship a fair shot.

"Logan?" Aunt Lou's voice broke the quiet. He steered the empty wheelbarrow toward the barn where his aunt stood. As he got closer, he saw worry etched in her expression. Logan double-timed it to the barn. Aunt Lou was tough, her expression cemented in a take-no-prisoners look from sunrise to sunset. Except right now.

"What happened?"

She held out her iPhone. "Cindy sent me the link this morning. It's a tabloid, but still, those pictures of you and Sadie look real, not some Photoshop creation like the bigfoot sightings."

Dread hit like the barrel of a gun to the side of his head. A hit he should have anticipated, but hadn't. Logan set the wheelbarrow aside and took his aunt's cell. The bookstore. The guesthouse front porch. Charlotte. Jesus Christ. These assholes had exploited a grieving little girl as if anyone who'd come into contact with him or Sadie was fair game. His grip tightened on the phone. He wanted to hunt them down and take them out. He wanted blood.

"Did she do this to you?" Aunt Lou demanded, her voice trembling, but fierce. She'd been his champion since he was in diapers—his mother, his family. But she couldn't fix this. He was pretty sure no one could.

"Did she use you?" his aunt asked.

"No."

But doubt clouded his vision as he handed the phone back to Aunt Lou. Sadie had been clear that her career came first. He'd respected her choice, welcoming the barrier to a serious relationship. And he knew her family and her childhood motivated her to succeed. He'd admired that about her. But he'd never considered how far she'd go to accomplish her goals. She'd told him point-blank that she'd tipped off a reporter who'd taken her picture in New York. But this? She wouldn't push these images out into the world. Would she?

"I need to talk to her," he said. "I'll come find you at the house. After."

Aunt Lou nodded. "I'm sorry, Logan. If I'd known who she was, I never would have rented her the guesthouse."

"I knew. And I trusted her." He shook his head, turning to the guesthouse, the bright sun mocking his foul mood. He needed to hear from Sadie that she hadn't done this.

Ten paces from the door, his cell vibrated in his pocket. He pulled it out, planning to ignore the call, thinking it was someone, probably a teammate, calling to ask what the hell he'd been thinking.

He glanced at the caller ID. It was someone calling to

ask that question—the one person he couldn't ignore, his commanding officer.

"Colonel."

"Since when does the definition of 'lying low' include getting pictures posted on the internet of some writer servicing you in a goddamn bookstore?" Lieutenant Colonel Walt Johnson barked.

Logan froze. He'd pictured the end of his career. More than he wanted to admit recently. But he'd assumed he'd be discharged for failing to do his job and getting his teammate shot, not for receiving a blow job.

"Did you know who she was when this happened?"

"No, sir." No lie there.

"This is a PR nightmare. Thank your lucky stars, son, that this online tabloid does not know your name or rank. If you are identified as a ranger, as one of the horse soldiers, you can kiss your career goodbye. Christ, you could face a court-martial for conduct unbecoming."

"Yes, sir." A court-martial, dishonorable discharge, all because a damn photographer had made a consensual, private moment public. And because he'd been too wrapped up in lust to ask the right questions. But, hell, who asked a writer visiting her pregnant sister if she expected photographers to follow her every movement?

"Get your ass back to base by eleven hundred tomorrow. Understood?"

"Yes, sir." The line went dead and Logan lowered the phone. He had one shot to keep his job and it all depended on Sadie shutting down this circus.

Logan marched up the front porch steps and knocked on her door. A second later, she answered, wearing her bathrobe. Beneath it, he saw her marines T-shirt peeking out. But her legs were bare and he guessed she wasn't wearing much else. An hour ago, before he'd seen those damning pictures, he would have scooped her up and carried her back to bed. He would have made love to her. Now, the idea seemed laughable.

"Logan." She stepped back, holding the door open. "Come in."

"Put on some pants, Sadie. We need to talk." Hands shoved in his pockets to keep from reaching out and touching her, he walked into the living room.

She closed the door. "I'll be right back."

A minute later, she reappeared wearing jeans and a fresh blue T-shirt. She'd drawn her long hair back in a tight bun.

"You've seen the pictures."

He nodded.

"Logan, I'm so sorry. I—"

"Did you know?" he ground out. "Was this all part of your plan to gain more publicity? Further your career?"

"No!"

"That photographer followed you for days, Sadie. And you never noticed?"

"He followed you, too," she shot back.

She had him there. All of his training and he'd failed to detect one slimy bastard with a camera. He probably deserved to lose his job.

"I would not intentionally ruin your career. I would never do that to you," she insisted. "You have to believe me."

He remembered the surprise on her face when she'd run from the house half-dressed and spotted the cameraman. She was driven to succeed. He knew that, but not at the expense of others. Aunt Lou had been wrong about that.

"I do," he said. "I believe you. Doesn't change the fact that this was a mistake. This fling."

"It's more than a fling," she said. "Last night—"

"I was wrong," he snapped.

She took his words like a slap to the face, recoiling, stepping away from him. And, Christ, he hated himself for lashing out. But this mess had exploded, dragging him to new lows.

"No, you weren't. I was there. We made love last night."

"Just because you didn't tie me up doesn't mean it was love, Sadie."

"You're right," she said quietly. "The sex doesn't prove anything. I can't offer you physical proof of how I feel. I like you, Logan." She shook her head. "No, it's more than that. I've fallen in love with you."

Logan let out a mirthless laugh. "I've been in love before. You don't ruin someone you love. You don't destroy them for personal gain."

He watched as tears welled in her eyes. "You lost your job."

"Not yet." But he had a feeling it was only a matter of time before he was told that after years of risking his life for his country and fighting for freedom in places that barely knew the meaning of the word, he was being sent packing with his tail between his legs.

"You know, I thought the worst thing that could happen was losing my wife and then allowing my grief to interfere with a mission and having that story shared with the world. But this is worse. Losing my career over a fucking blow job..." He shook his head.

"I'm going to fix this." Determination fought her tears and won. "I spoke with my publicist. I have an opportunity to go on national TV tomorrow morning and tell my side of the story."

"I'm returning to base in the morning. When I get there, I hope to still have a place on my team," he said. "You know how you can help with that? By doing me a favor and leaving me out of your interview."

She stepped toward him. "Logan—"

"Goodbye, Sadie."

He turned and headed for the door. This time, he knew walking away was the right thing to do, even if it felt like he was getting washed out to sea. And this time, he might drown.

21

SADIE SET HER princess wand on her sister's kitchen table. "I don't think I'll be needing this in New York."

Her bags were packed and loaded into the trunk of her rental car. She'd cleaned Lou's guesthouse from top to bottom, leaving behind a note and an envelope with cash to cover her father's stay.

He'd booked a flight right after they'd spoken this morning. She had a feeling he'd been ready for a while, his bags packed, and just needed to find the courage to ask for more money. He was arriving tonight, and she would miss him by hours. Her chance to have her family together, in one place, crushed by her career.

"How long before you have to leave?" Laurel asked, rocking her daughter in her arms. Sadie's niece had finally learned to sleep like a baby.

"I have an hour before I need to start driving."

Laurel nodded. "Plenty of time."

"For what?"

"Apple pie." Her twin gently set the sleeping baby in her bassinet and opened the fridge. "I sent Greg to The Quilted Quail for this after we saw the pictures."

"Laurel, you didn't have to," Sadie said.

"Yes, I did." She set the dish on the table with two forks. "Sit. Eat."

Sadie pulled out one of the wooden chairs and sat. "Thank you. You're right, I do need this."

"Look on the bright side," Laurel said. "At least we now have proof your sex life is more exciting than mine."

Sadie dug into the pie. "If that's the bright side, I'm screwed."

"What did Logan say?"

"He asked if I'd set the whole thing up for more publicity."

Laurel's fork froze in midair. "No."

"That hurt. A lot. I've never had anyone look at me and think 'ruthless.' But that's not the worst of it." She took a bite, forcing herself to taste the perfect combination of tart and sweet. "I told him I loved him."

"Love, like let's-get-married love?"

"More like I-want-to-see-you-again love. But either way it doesn't matter. He said I was wrong."

"What?" Laurel abandoned her fork in the dish, her arms resting on the table as she leaned forward.

"He has a point. He's been in love before. The kind you hope will last forever and ever. He would have walked away from his career for her. If I truly loved him, wouldn't I do the same? Say, to hell with the morning show and my career."

"What would that fix? The pictures are out there. If you do nothing, they'll keep hounding you."

Sadie closed her eyes. Her twin was right. They wouldn't go away quietly. Not now. If they'd discovered her staying in a small town, spending her days with her sister and writing, this never would have happened. Their pictures would have been too boring to make headlines.

But oral sex in a closed bookstore with a man who may or may not have a daughter? That was what tabloids lived for.

"Do the show," Laurel said. "But then, go after him. You always go after what you want. Don't let this be any different simply because it involves your heart instead of your job."

"What's the point? If he doesn't love me, if he still loves his late wife, why bother?"

"Do you believe that?"

Last night, in her bed, he'd made love to her. What they'd shared had nothing to do with kinky fantasies. He'd given her everything he had to give. She just couldn't say for sure if that included his heart.

"It doesn't matter what I believe. He's returning to Tennessee. He said goodbye and walked out the door without looking back." She scanned the rapidly disappearing pie. "What would going after him prove? That I failed at another relationship, only this time it broke my heart? Even if I was able to track him down on the military base, what would I say? If he doesn't believe me when I tell him I love him, what's left?"

Laurel reached out and took her hand. "Sometimes actions speak louder than words."

"That's my problem. Mine say I love my job. Loud and clear."

"Not always. You came here, didn't you? For me?"

"You're family."

"He could be, too, one day. If your heart is invested."

"It is. But I really wish it wasn't." Sadie stared at the half-empty dish, shaking her head as she pushed back from the table. "I should go before I eat the rest of this pie and show up for my television appearance five pounds heavier with dark circles under my eyes."

Laurel gave her a hug. "You'll be great tomorrow. I know you will."

Sadie nodded, blew a kiss to her sleeping niece and headed for her car. Tears flowed down her face as she drove past Lou's farm. Maybe if she cried the entire drive to New York, she'd stay dry-eyed during tomorrow's interview. This trip, falling for Logan, it had changed her. It had forced her to take a hard look at her priorities. But she still refused to cry in public.

She drove past Main Street Books, fighting back sobs. She'd been a fool to think she could have it all. Maybe some women could balance a thriving career and family, but she wasn't one of them. She'd tried and she'd failed, nearly costing the man she loved everything that was important to him.

"Another F," she murmured as she pulled onto the highway, "in the relationship column."

LOGAN HAULED HIS rucksack down the stairs to his aunt's kitchen, dressed in his uniform for the first time since he'd arrived on the farm. Through the window over the sink, he could see his aunt tossing hay bales into the front pastures, taking the time to stop and give her cows an affectionate pat. She'd appreciated his help while he was home. She'd told him as much when they'd said their goodbyes earlier. But he knew she'd be fine without him. For all her talk about wanting to live like a reality TV star, she loved her life here.

He opened the fridge and scanned the shelves for sandwich fixings, something he could take with him to eat on the way to the airport. He would have asked Aunt Lou to drive him, but he knew she hated long goodbyes. And despite her fiery personality, she drove so slowly he'd probably miss his flight.

He'd secured the last seat on the only flight to Nashville that day. If he didn't make it, he didn't have much chance of getting to Fort Campbell on time. After weeks of waiting, he was ready to be back where he belonged.

A knock sounded on the kitchen door.

"Shit." He finished spreading mayo on his bread, set the knife down and headed over to greet his aunt's friend, who'd undoubtedly stopped by for gossip. About him and those damn pictures.

Logan swung open the door. A tall man with red hair stood on the stoop, a large duffel at his feet. Though he looked younger than he probably was, Logan knew his identity without asking. He'd been out of the service for decades, but the man still carried himself like a marine.

"Afternoon, sir," Logan said.

Sadie's father held out his hand. "Tim Bannerman. I don't suppose you'd know where I can find my girls?"

"Sadie left. Headed back to New York. But Laurel should be home and she has your key." Aunt Lou had told him as much before she'd headed for the barn.

"I guess I'll make my way over to Laurel. If you wouldn't mind pointing me in the right direction."

Logan scanned the parking area and saw his truck parked beside his aunt's car. Sadie's dad must have cabbed it from the airport.

"I'm about to head out after I finish making this sandwich. I can give you a ride over there if you don't mind waiting." He stepped back, holding the door for the older man.

"Thank you." Mr. Bannerman stepped inside, carrying his bag as if it was featherlight. "Sorry I missed Sadie. It's been a long time since I've seen her."

"She had to get back to New York." For the interview

that could drive the last nail into the coffin currently holding his career.

"Dealing with the fallout from those pictures, I imagine," Mr. Bannerman said.

Logan looked up from his sandwich. "You've seen them?"

"Yes, son. I have." He held up his smartphone. "Sadie gave it to me last year. I can access the internet anywhere."

Logan knew everyone would see them. He was ready to face his teammates' teasing and the wide-eyed, probably disapproving looks from the people in Mount Pleasant. After all, it was their bookstore. But standing in front of this man, knowing he'd seen photographic evidence of his daughter on her knees, blowing him away—Christ, Logan wanted to sink into the floorboards.

"I'm sorry, sir." What else was there to say?

"Not your fault they showed up in the tabloids, was it?" Mr. Bannerman asked.

"No, sir."

Sadie's father nodded. "I didn't think so. My daughter's work—it lands her in funny places."

That was one way to look at it.

"But my daughter's job doesn't define her." The retired marine didn't look away. He stared at Logan as if assessing him from head to toe. "Wearing a uniform, I know more than most people how that can make you feel as if you live and die by your commitment to serve your country. I felt that way once upon a time. Then I met my wife and had my girls. I realized that the people you love, they're the ones who define who you are. When you make the hard choices—you make them for the people you love."

The older man's pristine posture slipped as if the weight of his life, and his regrets, rested heavily on him. "On the surface, I'm an unemployed veteran who spent most of his life getting by, going from one odd job to the next. I need my daughter's money to survive month to month. Without that…" He shook his head. From across the room, Logan could feel the shame radiating off the older man.

"I'd like to think I'm more than that to my daughters," he continued. "I gave them everything I had. All the love in my heart. Every day. Knowing that they might never be proud of me for the choices I made, but at least they'd feel loved."

The pieces fell into place. Sadie's unyielding drive, the way she understood Charlotte, even the reason she'd carried the pink wand her father had given her years ago while herding cows—it all made sense. She thought she was searching for stability and, yes, that played a role, but deep down he suspected she wanted to show her father that she loved him.

"You are more," Logan said. "You're her hero. And it has nothing to do with the uniform. You were her hero from the day she was born."

"I…" Sadie's father blinked, his posture straightening. "Thank you for that, son."

Logan nodded and picked up his sandwich. "How about I drive you over to Laurel's so you can meet your granddaughter?"

AN HOUR LATER, Logan sat in the long-term parking lot, staring at the terminal. Everything was in place for his return. He had a ticket. Aunt Lou had arranged for a friend to pick up his truck at the airport. In a few short hours, he'd be back where he belonged. He'd worked past his grief and found his way forward. He was ready to ship out with his team.

First, he'd have to face the fallout from the Sadie/MJ Lane scandal, but he hoped he could push past that obstacle. And part of him trusted Sadie to make things right, he realized. A woman who put her family first—she might not see it that way, but he knew it was the truth—she would not strip away another's career to sell more books. She would not drag an innocent child like Charlotte into the spotlight.

Sadie was her father's daughter through and through, her career choices driven by love. And like her dad, she believed she'd failed the people she loved most even when she was doing her best to help them.

Logan watched as a plane landed on the tarmac behind the terminal. He needed to get in there, clear security and catch his flight. He reached for the truck door, but didn't open it.

What drove his choices? On the surface, he was a soldier, a ranger who'd ridden a horse through Afghanistan and made one bad call during a mission. But who was he beneath that? There was honor and purpose in his job, but was it worth walking away from Sadie?

"Christ." He closed his eyes. He'd been here before, at the crossroads between love and duty. In the end, circumstances beyond his control had made the decision for him. This time it was on him. Did he go after the woman who lit up his life with her laughter, who turned him inside out with longing and who listened without pushing when he needed to unload?

What if he chose Sadie and went after her only to find out he wasn't ready to hand over his heart? The memory of Sadie demanding kisses, pulling him past his fears and hesitation reminded him that he wasn't alone in this. Together, they could find a way forward.

Logan let go of the door, reaching for the key still in the ignition. If he drove through the night, he'd reach New York City by morning. He pulled out his cell and dialed his commanding officer.

"Sir," he said quickly. "I need permission to go to New York City. That show is airing tomorrow morning and, sir, I need to be there."

"If you're worried about a court-martial, son—"

"No, sir. I'm worried about living the rest of my life knowing I walked away from a second chance at love."

22

THE SUN ROSE over Central Park, illuminating a sleepy New York City. At five-thirty in the morning, the sidewalks below her sixteenth-floor studio remained empty. The quiet didn't feel that different from Aunt Lou's farm in Mount Pleasant, even though Sadie knew it was a world away. In a few hours, the city streets would be overflowing with people rushing to work. She loved watching them from her perch above the city each day before she turned to her computer. But right now, she would rather hear the sound of cows mooing in the distance.

Don't think about it.

There was no going back now, only forward. Any minute the car service from the morning show would arrive and take her the few blocks to the studio. She was ready. She'd selected a simple green sundress for the interview. The fabric was soft and feminine and the color highlighted her eyes and red hair, which she'd pulled back into a simple twist. Not the bombshell outfit or diva hairstyle her publicist had recommended for her public debut. But then, she wasn't planning on giving them a sensational, headline-grabbing interview.

She'd stopped crying about an hour outside Mount

Pleasant last night. The long hours in the car had given her time to think. She'd realized that by striving to succeed for her family, she'd risked the thing she was trying to protect.

And that stopped today. She would do the interview and have her say, but after that she planned to slip away from the spotlight. Sadie Bannerman/MJ Lane would continue to write her books, but she would make it clear that the public was not welcome into the lives of the people she loved.

Her sister was right: Sadie always went after what she wanted. She wasn't afraid to use her voice. Now it was time to stand up for herself and demand that the people in those pictures maintain their privacy. If she wanted to go after Logan, she had to do this. Until she made room in her life for her loved ones, until she put them first, she didn't deserve him.

The phone on the wall rang. Sadie answered and told her doorman she would be right down. She was ready.

Ten minutes later, Sadie stepped out of the town car and walked into the studio. She smiled at her waiting publicist, who was already typing furiously on her phone.

"Good. You're here." Anne-Marie frowned. "I thought we decided on a black dress, something sultry, and your hair down."

"It's a 9:00 a.m. interview. I don't think sultry is appropriate."

"But you're MJ Lane."

"I'm also Sadie Bannerman. And she prefers this dress."

Realizing she'd lost, Anne-Marie led her down the hall to the makeup room. "Have you prepared your answers? Do we need to run through anything?"

"Yes. I'm prepared." Sadie didn't say another word,

instead focusing on the cheerful young woman intent on transforming her face.

At nine, Sadie took her seat opposite the friendly blonde morning show host, Kelsey Wise. The name, real or not, suited her. Ms. Wise looked sharp and focused. Determined.

Sadie smiled, knowing she was about to derail the host's plans. Ms. Wise might be shrewd and ready for battle, but Sadie was in love. And now Sadie knew that trumped ambition, work—everything.

"By now you've all seen the photographs plastered all over the web of the woman many believe to be MJ Lane, bestselling author of the book everyone has been talking about, *Isabelle's Command*. Well, we have her with us today. Please welcome Sadie Bannerman." Kelsey Wise paused, smiling like a cat about to pounce. "Ms. Bannerman, tell us, is it true you are MJ Lane?"

"Yes."

To her credit, Ms. Wise's smile remained in place when Sadie failed to elaborate.

"You have the people of America and many other countries around the world eagerly awaiting the second book in your series."

"The wait is almost over. Book two, *Isabelle's Command: Submission* releases next month. I think fans will be pleased with how the series's heroine finds her voice," Sadie said. This was the easy part, talking about her work. "In the third book, which I'm writing now, Isabelle comes into her own, unafraid to go after what she wants."

"And I assume what she wants is your bad-boy hero?"

"I see you've read the first book."

Ms. Wise raised her hand to her mouth as if admitting a secret. "I have."

"I think readers will be satisfied with Isabelle's transformation over the course of the books. She wants the hero, but she is not willing lose her sense of self to the relationship."

"Speaking of relationships..." Ms. Wise looked as if she was chatting with a girlfriend, but Sadie knew the hard part was coming. "Can you tell us more about the handsome man in those photographs?"

"No."

There was a beat of silence and Ms. Wise's eyes widened. She'd been promised a tell-all interview, not one-word answers. "Some of those images were quite erotic," the host continued. "Were you looking for inspiration?"

"No. I was looking for love. I didn't know it at first, but what you see in those pictures happens every day around the world. A girl falls in love with a boy." Hearing a slight waver in her voice, Sadie paused. She wanted her words to be loud and clear, no hesitation.

"Sometimes," she continued, "that leads to intimate moments. I think most people watching today will understand when I say that I expected those moments would remain private."

"But now that they're out there, for the world to see, can you tell us who the mystery man is?" Ms. Wise prompted, scrambling to save her interview.

"No."

Watching her exposé slip through her fingers, the host turned to the one question Sadie wanted to hear. "And the little girl?"

Sadie shook her head. "Nothing more than an example of a news outlet drawing false conclusions. The little girl lost her father in Afghanistan last year. The man in the pictures knew her father and took her out for ice cream. The only story there is sadness and loss. If the media wishes to delve deeper, perhaps they should highlight one of the charities that support children of fallen soldiers. Or look within their communities for children who might need a little extra cheering up, a chance to just be a kid after losing a parent on the battlefield."

The stunned expression on Ms. Wise's face said it all. Sadie had hit her mark, shutting down the hurtful chatter about Charlotte. They might still dig, and try to determine Logan's identity, but she felt saying more would only hurt, not help.

Sadie waited for the host to express her supposedly heartfelt sympathy for the girl in the picture. Instead, Ms. Wise raised her hand to her ear. Someone was feeding her information.

Nerves churned in Sadie's stomach for the first time. Had her answers backfired? She sat still, knowing there was little she could do now. Had someone behind the scenes discovered Logan's identity? What if they knew his name? His rank? The details behind his last mission?

Sadie forced herself to sit still when every bone in her body screamed, *Run.* Coming on this show, setting the record straight, had been a mistake. She'd failed on so many fronts. But she'd especially failed Logan. She'd tried to be his hero. To save him from losing everything he cared about. And judging from Ms. Wise's wide smile, Sadie had only made it ten times worse.

"It appears we have a special guest. The mystery man himself showed up at our door asking to speak with Ms. Bannerman." Kelsey Wise gave her a wink. "He's headed for the stage."

Logan. He was here. Hope surged through her. He'd come back. Again. This time, she refused to let him leave until she had her say. She had one chance to go after what she wanted—a future with the man she loved.

Sadie stood and squared her shoulders and held her head high. She was going for it. Right here. Right now. On national television.

23

LOGAN FOLLOWED THE security guard and the eager girl with the clipboard through the winding fluorescent underbelly of the news studio. Sadie was here somewhere. He had to talk to her. Now. He was running out of time.

His commanding officer had given him a brief respite. Less than forty-eight hours. By this time tomorrow morning, he had to report for duty. Logan had every intention of securing his future with Sadie before the deadline.

The hallway ended, letting out into a bright open space. The stage, he realized, where they filmed the show. Lights and cameras surrounded the room's perimeter. In the center was a raised dais with an L-shaped sofa and a coffee table. In front of the sofa, Sadie stood beside a blonde woman who looked as if she was made of plastic.

"Ladies and gentlemen," the blonde said with a wide smile, "please welcome U.S. Army Ranger Logan Reed."

The words crossed her lips and Logan knew he'd walked into an ambush. He had about two seconds before the cameras and lights turned his way and broadcast his image into homes across the country. He had two choices, run for the hall and hope to hell he could save his career, or do what he'd come here to do—talk to Sadie.

Logan stepped into the light. "Sadie—"

"Wait." She held up her hand. He watched as Sadie moved around the coffee table. She approached him, her green sundress dancing around her legs, reminding him of the dress she'd worn to the Summer Festival. She stopped within arm's reach. With her long hair pulled back into some sort of twist, and makeup accentuating her face, she looked beautiful. But then, he'd thought she was gorgeous with dirt smudged on her cheek in a cow field. From the moment he'd met her, Sadie had radiated light, laughter and a sex appeal that had him wrapped around her finger.

She leaned toward him, dropping her voice to a whisper. "You don't have to do this. Not here."

Logan widened his stance, rooting his feet to the ground. "I'm not walking away, Sadie. Not this time."

"All right, then." She stepped back, straightening her spine. "I have something I'd like to say."

He was aware of the cameras, the lights and the blonde on the stage, but none of it mattered. Only Sadie mattered. She was his world, his future. He nodded for her to continue.

"I know you were married to a great woman and you loved her. You would have risked everything for her," she said. "I'm not asking you to make that choice. If you think you can make room in your heart for me, I want to be with you. Wherever you need to be, I'm there. I'll wait for you while you deploy. And I promise I'll stand by you. I'm strong. I can take the waiting. I can make this work. I have faith in you, in myself and in us. Over time, we can make this work."

He didn't doubt her strength. Not anymore. She'd move mountains for the important people in her life. He knew that now. "If you give me a chance—"

"Please, let me finish," she said. "I made a mistake.

A series of them, really. I put my career first, before the people I care about. Success—I thought it was everything. And I was wrong."

Logan shook his head and stepped closer, taking her hands in his. "Sadie, everything you do is for your family. Don't you see that? I love that about you."

The determination shining in her eyes faltered, revealing her uncertainty.

He nodded. "Yesterday, when I saw those pictures," he continued, "I was running scared. Not just of what the media attention meant for my job, but of my feelings for you. In a short time, they've exploded. I've fallen for you, Sadie. I love you."

"You do?"

He nodded. "Yes. I love *you,* Sadie Bannerman. Not your job. Not MJ Lane. You. And I want to be with you."

Her brow furrowed. "But what about your career? Those pictures—"

"Are of a private moment between two people who care deeply for each other. Nothing wrong with that."

Doubt continued to cloud her face. "Your commanding officer agrees?"

"He doesn't control every part of my life," he said. "And at the end of the day, you're more important. You're my future."

"And you're mine."

Tears welled in her eyes. She tried to fight them, to stop the trembling in her limbs, but it was a losing battle. Logan's hands on hers were the only thing holding her steady. Logan, the man who'd declared his feelings for her in front of thousands of people.

Through her tears, she looked into his eyes and saw the truth. He was here. For her. And he loved her.

"Logan, I know we've only known each other a few

days. But in your world, a few days is sometimes all you have. I know what I feel. I know what is in my heart. I love you and I want to build a life with you. I want to be the one waiting for you when you come home. Always."

Wrapping her arms around his neck, she leaned forward and touched her lips to his, kissing him with all her heart. Let America watch. Let them judge. She'd found her fairy-tale ending, her happily-ever-after. Nothing else mattered.

Epilogue

IT WAS LATE. Nearly midnight. Sadie sat in the team room waiting, surrounded by wives, girlfriends, fathers, mothers and children who'd been allowed to stay up way past their bedtime for this special occasion.

Homecoming.

"Is he here yet?" a small boy, maybe four, demanded, running up to the woman seated beside Sadie at the rectangular table.

"Not yet," his mother said with a smile. "Soon."

The boy, who'd been fighting sleep but now seemed to have found his second, or maybe third wind, nodded. "Can we eat the cake while we wait?"

"No, honey. That's for your father."

A large rectangular cake frosted red, white and blue sat in the center of the table. On top it read Welcome Home.

Sadie drew her sweater tight around her, fighting off the chill. It was cold, even for December, with temperatures dipping into the twenties. Sadie had hoped the weather would be warmer in Clarksville compared to New York, but either way it didn't matter. There was no place she'd rather be. Especially tonight.

This was her first time welcoming Logan home from a

deployment. He'd been gone four months, leaving weeks after their national TV appearance. The army had welcomed him back with open arms. And there had never been so much as a whisper about a court-martial for unbecoming conduct. Apparently, a woman in love declaring she would wait for her soldier while he fought for his country generated mountains of positive publicity.

She suspected there would be a downside to the publicity, too. Logan had dropped hints in the days before he'd deployed, while they were still setting up house at the base, that he'd probably be assigned to the "log train" team. Instead of leading the charge, he'd be at the base arranging for supplies and providing support. Not as exciting, but as he pointed out, there was no small job when it came to his missions. Everything they did over there was important. He'd told her again and again, when she'd pushed him to tell his commanding officer that the bad guys probably didn't read the tabloid reports about erotica authors or watch morning shows, that he felt lucky to be back with his team. He'd do whatever was asked of him. No questions. No complaints.

Sadie had a feeling she'd never know one way or the other if his commanding officer had kept him on the base or sent him into battle. Whatever the mission, wherever he'd gone, he wouldn't speak of it.

The little boy's mother leaned toward Sadie, pulling her back into the present—the team room, and the quiet family-only homecoming awaiting Logan and his team. No media or marching bands for the Special Forces soldiers.

"I read that book," the woman said. "The one everyone is talking about."

For once, she was not referencing an MJ Lane title. This time the book belonged to Professor Margaret Barlow.

"It's a great account of the horse soldiers' ride," Sadie replied, offering her stock answer.

The woman nodded. "It was nice to read a story that made the men seem human. And I was glad she did not harp on your boyfriend's mistake. In the end, no one died and they rescued three aid workers. One error does not change the fact that he's a hero."

"I agree," Sadie said. "Though I could do without women coming up to me in the supermarket and telling me they wanted to give my boyfriend a big old hug when they read about how he was trying to juggle grief and his duty to his country."

The woman laughed, but the sound was quickly drowned out by footsteps in the hall. The soldiers were home. Everyone in the room rose and children rushed to the door. With one hand, Sadie held up the sign she'd made, wrapping the other around the small gift she'd brought.

Men poured in, their faces lined with exhaustion and relief. They found their loved ones, gathering them close, holding on tight. The room filled with *welcome home*s and *I love you*s. The small boy demanded they cut the cake.

Sadie scanned the crowd until finally she found him bringing up the rear. Logan. Mr. Ruggedly Handsome. Her soldier. Her love.

"Sadie." He gathered her in his arms, holding her close. She felt his chest expand as he inhaled. "You smell good. So damn good. Like home."

She wrapped her arms around him, drawing him tight against her. After all these months, seeing him, knowing he was safe—she didn't have the words. It was better than apple pie, better than orgasms, though she might reconsider the second point once she got him home. Which reminded her…

"I have a present for you." She drew back, until she could see his face. "Hold out your hand."

He did as he was told and Sadie pressed the spool of pink ribbon into his palm. "Are you ready to follow orders, soldier?"

Logan laughed, his eyes sparkling as he pulled her closer and lowered his lips to hers. He kissed her long and hard. When he finally allowed her to catch her breath, he kept his forehead pressed to hers.

"Sadie Bannerman, I'm yours to command."

* * * * *

COMING NEXT MONTH FROM

HARLEQUIN®

Blaze

Available August 19, 2014

#811 A SEAL'S FANTASY
Unrated!
by Tawny Weber
Navy SEAL Dominic Castillo has a reputation for always getting the girl—but he meets his match when forced to protect Lara Banks, the tempting, unrepentant sister of his rival.

#812 BEHIND CLOSED DOORS
Made in Montana
by Debbi Rawlins
Sexy rancher Nathan Landers steers clear of Blackfoot Falls and the small-town rumor mill, but beautiful newcomer Bethany Wilson is offering a naughty no-strings deal he can't refuse!

#813 CABIN FEVER
The Wrong Bed
by Jillian Burns
On a cruise, fashion blogger Carly Pendleton tries to fight her attraction to "Average Joe" contest winner Joe Tedesco, who sizzles with raw masculinity. They don't seem to have much in common...but can she fight the fire blazing between them?

#814 STRIPPED DOWN
Pleasure Before Business
by Kelli Ireland
One impulsive night with gorgeous dancer Dalton Chase leaves engineer Cassidy Jameson aching for more. But inviting him into her bed is one thing...inviting him into her life, quite another.

HBCNM0814

REQUEST YOUR FREE BOOKS!
2 FREE NOVELS PLUS 2 FREE GIFTS!

HARLEQUIN

Blaze

red-hot reads!

YES! Please send me 2 FREE Harlequin® Blaze™ novels and my 2 FREE gifts (gifts are worth about $10). After receiving them, if I don't wish to receive any more books, I can return the shipping statement marked "cancel." If I don't cancel, I will receive 4 brand-new novels every month and be billed just $4.74 per book in the U.S. or $4.96 per book in Canada. That's a savings of at least 14% off the cover price. It's quite a bargain. Shipping and handling is just 50¢ per book in the U.S. and 75¢ per book in Canada.* I understand that accepting the 2 free books and gifts places me under no obligation to buy anything. I can always return a shipment and cancel at any time. Even if I never buy another book, the two free books and gifts are mine to keep forever.

150/350 HDN F4WC

Name _____ (PLEASE PRINT) _____

Address _____ Apt. # _____

City _____ State/Prov. _____ Zip/Postal Code _____

Signature (if under 18, a parent or guardian must sign)

Mail to the Harlequin® Reader Service:
IN U.S.A.: P.O. Box 1867, Buffalo, NY 14240-1867
IN CANADA: P.O. Box 609, Fort Erie, Ontario L2A 5X3

Want to try two free books from another line?
Call 1-800-873-8635 or visit www.ReaderService.com.

* Terms and prices subject to change without notice. Prices do not include applicable taxes. Sales tax applicable in N.Y. Canadian residents will be charged applicable taxes. Offer not valid in Quebec. This offer is limited to one order per household. Not valid for current subscribers to Harlequin Blaze books. All orders subject to credit approval. Credit or debit balances in a customer's account(s) may be offset by any other outstanding balance owed by or to the customer. Please allow 4 to 6 weeks for delivery. Offer available while quantities last.

Your Privacy—The Harlequin® Reader Service is committed to protecting your privacy. Our Privacy Policy is available online at www.ReaderService.com or upon request from the Harlequin Reader Service.

We make a portion of our mailing list available to reputable third parties that offer products we believe may interest you. If you prefer that we not exchange your name with third parties, or if you wish to clarify or modify your communication preferences, please visit us at www.ReaderService.com/consumerschoice or write to us at Harlequin Reader Service Preference Service, P.O. Box 9062, Buffalo, NY 14269. Include your complete name and address.

HB13R2

Entering her building, Lara felt the weight of the day on her shoulders. She still had hours of homework and eight shows to dance over the weekend. If she nailed this assignment, she'd have the top grade in the class, which meant an internship with a top-flight security firm.

Six more weeks to go. With a sigh, she rounded the hallway to her corridor.

Lara Lee, Cyber Detective.

She grinned, then blinked. Frowning, she noted the hall lighting was out. She'd just put her key in the lock when she felt him.

It wasn't his body heat that tipped her off.

Nope, it was the lust swirling through her system, making her knees weak and her nipples ache.

Taking a deep breath, she turned. "Do you always lurk in the shadows?"

"Hall light is out. Shadows are all you've got here."

"What do you want?"

"I told you. I need to talk to you about your brother."

"And I told you. I don't have a brother."

Not anymore.

"Lieutenant Phillip Banks. Navy SEAL. Ring any bells?" His words were easy, the look in his eyes as mellow as the half smile on his full lips.

"My last name is Lee." Then, before she could stop herself, she asked, "Why are you running errands for this guy, anyway?"

His dark eyes flashed. "Sweetheart, do I look like anyone's errand boy?" he said.

Lara couldn't resist.

She let her eyes wander down the long, hard length of his body. Broad shoulders and a drool-worthy chest tapered into flat abs, narrow hips and strong thighs.

She wet her lips and met his eyes again.

He looked hot.

As if he'd like to strip her down and play show-and-tell.

Tempting, since she'd bet that'd would be worth seeing.

"Sorry," she said. "I'm not the woman you're looking for."

Damn.

Not for the first time in his life, Dominic Castillo cursed Banks. The guy was a pain. Figured that long, lean and sexy was just as bad.

He wanted to grab her, haul her off to the nearest horizontal surface.

Insane.

He was on a mission. *She* was his duty.

He'd never lusted after a mission before.

Pick up A SEAL'S FANTASY by Tawny Weber, available in September 2014 wherever you buy Harlequin® Blaze® books.